Luvin' ON A COLD HITTA

EBONY DIAMONDS

© 2020
Published by Ebony Diamonds

PASSION SANTINA

"Nope, get the fuck out, Chino. Swear, I'm done."

I marched through our townhouse in North Philly throwing everything of his I could find. You know this man came in there trying to tell me he had a bitch pregnant, but he wanted us to meet and be cool. Yeah, I been with this nigga for six years, and he still wasn't shit. That was my bad, though. I should have been sent his dumb ass packing when I got smarter. The fucked up part was if I did, I wouldn't have shit, and that seemed to be where I was heading unless I went back home, which I didn't wanna do.

My parents hated Chino, and I fought tooth and nail to be with his ass. I could hear my parents now saying *I told you so.*

"You overreacting as usual. The bitch got pregnant when you kicked me out for three months. You thought I wasn't getting me a nut or two? You got life fucked up, shorty. Stop

1

throwin' shit, and sit your ass down for a minute. We wasn't together at that point." He pulled on my arm and kissed my, neck causing me to break down and cry.

I got me some dick when we broke up but I damn sure didn't get pregnant.

"Why? Just why, my nigga? I mean, what the fuck be goin' through that stupid fuckin' head when you do me like this? Well, look tho, you a free man, homie. You make me sick." I got up and finished tossing his shit around.

"Passion, on God, if you don't clean this shit up and shut the fuck up, a fist print gonna be your new makeup. Stop the theatrics because me and you both know your ass ain't going no damn where. Now sit your ass here and tell me I'm a lie." He waited for me to respond.

"I hate you so much." I fell on the couch and covered my face with my hands.

"I love you though, ma. I swear I do," he begged, holding onto my hands.

"Not like I deserve," I said then got up and walked into the room. I lay across the bed with a nothing but sadness and pathetic bitch syndrome weighing me down.

He was right. I leave and then come back because I had nobody and nothing, which was all my own doing. I always thought I would save up money and leave, but he gave me so much I couldn't get on my own. Now, I wasn't your average piece of hood ass. I grew up fancy and shit, but when I was fifteen, I let a nigga sweet talk me out my drawers, and that nigga was this nigga. I always had fantasies of being some gangster's girl and shit, but I swear I wish I would have just listened to my parents when they told me to stay on our side of town. Now, here I was, three miscarriages and a hundred heartaches later. But shit, a bitch still standing, and you can't take that shit from me.

All my other friends went on to live dreams while Passion was twenty-one, and her life ain't shit. I needed better, and this shit was getting worse and worse.

"I'll leave for now until you cool off, but I'm coming back, baby," he said and walked out the house.

I smoked and drank a whole bottle of X then went the fuck to sleep so I wouldn't have to feel the pain.

After a few hours, I heard the alarm let me know that somebody was entering the house,

"Baby." Chino walked into the room.

"What?" I cut my eyes at him.

He sat on the bed and handed me a black, square box. I knew it was just another pay off for my heartbreak.

"You can't buy me, Chino." I set the box down without opening it.

"Passion," he said in a stern voice.

I exhaled deeply and picked the box up to open it. When I did, I couldn't hide my smile, but looking at the bronzed picture of us on our first date still couldn't erase the emptiness and worthlessness I felt.

"You said you would love me forever, ma, come on," he said, repeating the same line he often hit me with.

I laid back and let the tears slid from my eyes and into my earlobes.

"I just wanna go back to sleep, Chino. Please, just go back on the streets and do whatever you do with whoever you do it with."

"Fuck, Passion, damn. One day I'ma just say fuck it too," he had the nerve to say.

"Nigga, you been saying fuck it and doing you, so what fuckin' difference would that shit make?"

"Aight, man." He got up and rolled out, slamming the door behind him.

I called Cherry. She was my closest friend and my confidant. I hated to do it because she was so tired of hearing about me continuing this cycle that she barely listens. I mean, why would she want to hear about my minimal shit when she was going through her shit?

The call went straight to voicemail, and there was nothing left for me to do but go to sleep.

I HADN'T SEEN Chino in a week, and that was cool by me. I needed my space, and I kind of felt good. Today, I was on the way to get my hair done, and then I was going shopping. I got to my stylist, Shawn, and sat right in his chair.

"Ohhh, chile, I see you on time for once." He cracked his back and put on his yellow smock.

"Shut up, I'm always on time." I giggled.

"Look at them bags, honey. Ain't no nigga worth the stress." Shawn looked at my face.

"I already know, that's why I kicked his ass out," I said.

"Yeess, bitch, yess. Finally. Now you know my cousin Bo been on your heels since he dropped his girl off here that day," he said excitedly.

"Nigga, he dropped his woman off and tried to holla at me. Why would I want a nigga like that?" I said as I sat at the bowl.

"Bitch, fuck love. Get money. That's my cousin, so I know how he roll, and ole boy stacked up." He twerked.

"Nah, I'm good." I Laughed.

For the next six hours we did what most women do in a shop and talked shit with some good gossip. I was glad he was done, though, because my ass was starting to feel numb. I felt my new Remy fall down my back. As always, he did the bomb job.

I grabbed my card out my purse and handed it to Shawn. While he ran my card, I talked to Ginny, the stylist next to him.

"It's declinin'," Shawn yelled loud enough or everybody to hear.

"Damn you screamin' it. Let me check my account, but, of course,it should be plenty." I rolled my eyes at him.

I went into my app for PNC and saw it had a balance of $12.00. Nah, this shit can't be right. I had over forty-five thousand in this one alone. That was just my hair fund card. I checked my other account and it was empty. What the fuck? Then it dawned on me. Chino.

I called his phone, and he answered.

"Wassup." He answered like nothing was wrong.

"My accounts are empty. You knew that tho, right?" I said ready to cry if he did this to me.

"I mean, you said you want me to go, so I went. I ain't think you was gon' be mad. This what you wanted, right?" he responded.

I hung, went into my purse, pulled out a stack, and took off 2500 dollars, which I handed to Shawn. I was gonna use that to go to the casino later, but I couldn't do shit because I was flat broke. Chino had reached an all time low with this one.

"Bitch, you want Bo's number or not?" Shawn said with that 'bitch you betta' look.

"Hell no. Fuck niggas," I said and stomped out.

I didn't even go back home. I just drove until I reached Cherry's row house in the badlands. I needed to talk to her ass. When I pulled up, I stopped when I saw Chino's car sitting on the corner. My heartbeat started to slow down, and I hoped this wasn't what I thought it was. I pulled up fast right in front of her house and banged on the door.

"Cherry!" I banged harder and started kicking it.

She swung the door open and looked at me like I was crazy. I looked down the street and saw Chino coming out of a house with two dudes. When she saw what I was looking at, she went off.

"Oh, bitch, I know you ain't think nobody was fuckin' that community dick ass nigga of yours. You know what? Fuck you, Passion. Keep your drama and failed ass relationship to yourself." She slammed the door right in my face.

I ran down the stairs before Chino saw me, but I was too late. He was already walking in my direction.

"You came to talk shit to your bucket head ass friend." He walked up and reached for me.

"Fuck you, Chino. You embarrassed the shit out of me today. Why you gotta be the way you are? You used to love me." I went to my car, and he stopped me.

"I'll give it all back. I'm sorry. I was a fuck nigga for that. I just can't let you leave. You know you my heart." He reached in the window and grabbed my hand.

"I hate to see how you treat an enemy if this how you treat somebody you love. I'm goin' home, Chino."

I rolled the window up and sped off down the street. I kind of wondered who those niggas were that he was down the street with because I had never seen them, but I wasn't about to worry about Chino's ass no more. Fuck him.

CHINO LUVHER

"So, you went right ahead begging that bitch back, right? I swear you so fuckin' stupid for her." Cherry said, sitting on the edge of her bed.

I swear I was a fast ass nigga. I ran down in some nigga's house when Passion came knocking on the door. I paid them to act like I was coming out the front.

"That's my girl. I don't know why you act like you stupid or something. I'ma always want her back." I grabbed the blunt off the floor that I had rolled right before Passion showed up.

I went ahead and put all her money back in her account. I guess I called myself trying to show her I didn't have to give her shit, but I felt bad as fuck because she ain't never did shit for me to treat her like that.

"Then go ahead and run home after her. Y'all both stupid." She got a lighter and handed it to me.

"Bitch, you just mad because I love her and not your ass. You got some good pussy, though, that's straight facts right there," I said and tickled her pussy through her shorts.

"Stop," she snapped and pushed me.

"I want you to just leave her for good. You got me and your son living like fuckin' nobodies and shit," she said, referring to our three year old son Ronnie.

"Well, I told you not to have him because I wasn't gonna be with you, but you wanted to. I'm glad you did because I love him. You act like I don't keep y'all straight, tho." I reminded her how she don't even have to work.

"Nigga, we live in the badlands, why we can't live like you and Passion? Type of shit is that?" she asked and lay back on the couch.

"I'm sorry, aight. But we are what we are, ma. Fuck buddies," I said, getting up to leave because I knew she was about to do shows and shit.

"Where you goin'?" she asked, standing with me.

"Home, I'm boutta go try to talk to Passion and love on my shorty." I pulled out some money and set it on the table. "Take my son shopping.'"

"Just stay gone, Chino." She started crying.

I shook my head and left because she put herself in this situation by fucking her friend's nigga and catching feelings. In all honesty, I loved Passion, but it was like I couldn't stop myself sometimes. Now this shit with Cherry had to stop because we too deep in, and I felt that Cherry was gon' break soon and start some shit.

I jogged down the stoop and walked down the street to my car. As soon as I saw it, I got pissed, but I gave Passion that one. She busted my windows out. My guilt couldn't let me be mad at her.

I called my homeboy, Lox, and asked him to come scoop a nigga. Geico was on the way to get my shit, and I was happier than hell when I saw Lox pulling up with a quickness.

"What's good, Slime." I dapped him up, and he sped off.

"What happened to your whip?" he asked as he hit the corner.

"Passion, man. She be lunchin', bruh," I said like she didn't have a reason to be mad.

"That's crazy, man. Well, look, you know you got that other whip you hold at shorty's joint if you want me to drop you there," he offered.

"Yup, that's the move," I said.

We talked shit as we headed to my friend, Sade's house. She was just a cool bitch. I only fucked her once, and since the pussy was trash, I was over her. So, we been cool ever since. Bitch would take a charge for me, and that's why I kept her around.

I saw Cherry calling my phone, but I shook my head and ended it. I was gonna fall back; she wasn't about to make me lose Passion.

"Nigga yeah, I need a few more of them chickens, and make 'em fat bitches," I told True as I handed him his money in an orange duffle.

This nigga had that dirty raw, and it helped that he was my cousin. I needed that shit if I was gonna keep fucking these blocks up.

"Nigga, stop talkin' like I don't bless your dingy ass. Just be at the pick up." True walked off and jumped in his whip.

I left and headed straight to Zales to pick up this chain for Passion. It had been two weeks, and she was still home with me, so I felt like that was a start. I loved her so much, and I just wanted her to feel it. As I walked in, I took out the knot of money and slid it toward the clerk who I saw last time. Bitch tried to play me like I was broke until I kept spending money in this bitch. Hoe tried to come at me, and I blocked her gold digging ass. Now every time I come get something for Passion, she's always salty.

"How you doin'? I came to grab my shorty some diamonds. What new shit y'all got?" I asked, looking into one of the cases. The whole top row had these pink diamonds. I wanted that

"I see you eying our Pink Princess collection." The corny ass manager walked up, basically moving the associate out the way to get the commission.

"Yeah, I like that bracelet and that heart ring." I pointed out my two choices.

"Okay, will you need the ring altered?" he asked.

"Nah." I opened my phone and called Passion to see if she was hungry.

"Yeah," she answered, sounding all sad and shit.

"I'm boutta go grab some cheese steaks, you hungry?"

"Yeah, and bring me a pop. And a Snickers."

"Whatever you want. Matter of fact, get dressed so we can go out. Fuck a cheese steak, we goin' to Ruth's Chris. Be there in a minute."

I hung up and waited for them to bring my baby's shit down. I was about to just blow bags on Passion today and try to put some smiles on her face. Yeah, she deserved a nigga better than me, but I loved her, and I still wanted her.

"You sure you don't wanna get it sized?" The manager came back with the paper work.

"Nah, I'ma see if she can fit it, and if she can't, I can get it resized," I told him as I looked at the prices and tried to calculate with tax how much it would be. I peeled off 90 fresh 100 dollar bills.

"Okay, Michele is gonna wrap that up for you." He pointed at the salty bitch.

She got my shit and handed the bag over.

"Until next time I fuck up." I laughed and walked out then got in my car.

I drove home so I could take Passion out and try to put a smile on her grill. I didn't want her hurting, and I was the once who caused it. She definitely deserved better than me.

"I'm back, ma." I opened the door to our three story townhouse in Roxborough.

I heard Passion walking down the ivory stairs. Once she got to the landing, I smiled hard as hell. She looked pretty than a motherfucker in a two piece black halter set with some sexy ass heels. Her body was perfect, and I couldn't wait to hit that shit if she gon' let me.

"You look beautiful, bae." I hugged and kissed her cheek.

"Thank you," she said and sat on the couch.

"I got you this." I handed her the latest to her diamond collection.

"Thanks." She took it without emotion and opened it.

"It's a pinky ring." I took it out and slid it on her finger. Then I put the necklace on and diamond bracelet.

"It's pretty." She smiled.

"You pretty ma." I slipped my tongue into her mouth, and she kissed me back.

"Chino, I think we need a break," she blurted out.

"What? What the fuck you mean we need a break?" I barked.

"You don't want a relationship, you just want me." She looked like she was done.

"That's fucked up, shorty. You got me thinkin' we about to go out and have a good time, and it was some goodbye shit tho?" I said, feeling myself get pissed off.

"We can still go out. I would think that after six years you would've learned to stop disrespecting me and our relationship but no, you haven't, and I'm done." She started crying.

"Aye, fuck all that cryin' shit. Your ass ain't leavin' me, ma. You know I can't let you do that." I got down on my knees and grabbed her hands.

"Chino, you do this every time. Over the last week, I thought maybe I could deal with what you keep doin' since you can't stop, but what kind of weak bitch would that make me?" She looked dead into my eyes, and I knew she was serious.

"So, what you gon do? Take my fuckin' money with you?" I barked and got up.

"No, if you wanna take everything, that's fine. But I was gon' go see my folks," she said.

"Yo, this is shit fucked up." I walked away and knocked over the lamp then threw the table at the wall. Her family was rich, and I knew she ain't need my damn money if they let her back in.

"Stop, Chino!" she cried.

"No, I ain't gon' fuckin' stop shit. You ain't leavin' me, so shut up." I grabbed her up and kissed her roughly. "Please, Passion." I felt on her ass, and she tried to push my hands off, but I over powered her.

"Chino, listen." She started breathing heavily when I touched her pussy through her thin underwear. I ripped off the fabric and pushed my finger into her tight pussy.

"I luh yo ass, shorty. You can't leave me." I kissed her long and hard then pulled my dick out.

I picked her up and slowly slid her on it. She was soaked; yeah, she wanted the dick.

"Fuck. Baby, why you keep hurtin' me?" She moaned and cried.

"I don't know. Let me make you feel good baby, shhh."

I pulled her bottom lip into my mouth and pressed her against the wall. She wrapped her legs around my waist, and I cuffed her shoulders and drilled into Passion hard until she started cumming. She had that cum all night pussy, and that shit would get pool wet. We never left. We ended up going upstairs and falling asleep.

"YOU KNOW you really need to tell Passion about him." My mother looked at me and Ronnie as we sat across from her at the table.

"I know she gon leave me, ma. I can't," I explained.

"Why stall the inevitable? You treat that child so bad and wanna cry that you love her. She the dumb one." She shook her head.

"Damn, I'm your fuckin' son. Be on my side," I snapped.

"Bitch." She swung and smacked me in the back of the head. "Just who the fuck you talkin' to?"

"I'm sorry, Ma," I said, ready to knock her fucking teeth out.

"I said what the fuck I said, and deep down, you know the fuck I'm right," she spat.

"Aight, man. We about to roll." I jumped up.

"Nigga, I cooked all this food, and fuck a anger issue,

you gon' eat it. Now sit down and let him eat, dumb ass," she said.

I rolled my eyes and picked up my beer.

"I ain't know you was here." My father came in.

"Yeah," I simply stated. He was a drunk ass nigga half the time.

"My grandboy." He hi fived Ronnie and almost fell. He smelled like a fifth.

"You need to sit down, Pops," I said.

"You sit down," he said and took a seat anyway.

"You been watching the games?" I asked.

My father loved Basketball.

"Yeah, I put money on Lebron bitch ass. He betta come through." He laughed.

"How you put money on anything? You ain't got shit. You mean I put money on it," my mother said in a nasty tone.

Here we go.

"Bitch, fuck you and your dry ass pussy. That's why I don't fuck you no more. Your mouth turns me the fuck off," he shot back.

"Aww, Granddaddy said a bad word." Ronnie covered his ears.

"Can y'all stop for a minute?" I asked while my mother set me and Ronnie's plates down.

"Fuck him and his uncircumcised dick. My pussy stays wet, mufucka, ask Brady down the street, bitch." My mother motioned to her pussy, and I was done.

"Come on." I got up, grabbed Ronnie, and left with out even eating.

They made me sick with that shit, couldn't stop fighting for shit.

I went to Cherry's house to drop Ronnie back off, and I saw Passion's car.

"Fuck," I said.

I called her to see if she was leaving soon.

"Hey," she answered dryly.

"Wassup, baby? I miss you, I think we should get some lunch," I said, heading McDonald's for Ronnie since she was there.

"Okay, that's fine Chino." She wasn't excited at all. my baby was unhappy and wasn't shit I could do to change the shit right now.

"Just come home, I'ma be there soon," I said but she was silent. "Please." I added.

"Okay, I'm on the way," she said.

"Love you," I got out before she hung up.

I got Ronnie's food and took the back streets back to Cherry's house to make sure I ain't come across Passion.

Once I made it back, Cherry wanted to pick a fight, of course.

"Why the fuck you gotta call her when she here? You know I hate that shit," she screamed.

"You just mad cuz we goin' out. I know she told you," I said, walking out her room.

"Chino, on some real shit. I can't do this shit no more," Cherry started with that same speech.

"Yeah, then tomorrow you'll be texting for me to come over. Please shut up and let me leave," I said as she blocked my exit.

"No, you ain't fuckin' leaving to go home and treat her like a fuckin' princess and kissing ass cuz you fucked up again. And who is the bitch you got pregnant?"

"None of your business. You ain't my girl." I pushed her out the way and quickly left out the front door.

"Fuck you, Chino. I'ma call Passion and tell her everything," she said out the front door.

I ran back up the stairs.

She tried to close the door, but I burst through and she fell on the floor.

"Tell her what?" I went down and slapped the shit out of her.

"Stop it." She tried to crawl, but I stepped on her foot.

"Tell her what, bitch?" I popped her in the side of the face.

"Help me!" Cherry started screaming, and Ronnie came down the stairs.

"We just playin', man. Daddy gon' see you later, okay." I went over and kissed him, and he hugged me.

"Stay away from me, Chino." Cherry said as I left and closed the door.

I wasn't about to play stupid games with no bitch. That revenge shit gon' get her ass killed.

PASSION

"So, you decided to stay, huh? You like that shit, don't you?" my older sister, Alex, said and smacked her teeth.

"No, I don't like shit. I just don't know if I'm welcome at Ma and Dad's house."

"Of course, you are. You the one who ran off and jumped on the first hood rat you could find." She rolled her eyes.

My sister looked just like our mother, a young Angela Basset in the flesh.

"Ohh, bitch, you so annoyin'. That stuck up ass attitude just makes my ass itch." I rolled my eyes at her.

"Makes your ass itch?" She giggled.

My sister took advantage of that snooty ass up bringing and irritated my soul when she acted like this. Bitch even got her a white husband.

"You aggy as fuck, man." I got up and threw a hundred on the table.

"You're so sensitive. I was telling Mark the other day about how I wished we could be closer." She looked at me.

"We could if you didn't have to look your nose down on everybody who didn't grown up like we did. I was gonna ask you to go out tonight, but I don't want my ghetto ass to embarrass you."

"Passion, stop." She came up behind me, and I turned around.

"What, man?" I folded my arms.

"Let's do that. We can go out tonight," she said.

"Aight."

I walked out and got into my car. I was serious about me and Chino taking a break, and just because I didn't move out yet didn't mean shit. I was about to put my CNA certificate to use. Fuck it, I wasn't about to fully depend on anybody else. Chino needed to know I could live without his ass for once.

When I pulled up to the house, I saw a vehicle I didn't recognize parked in the driveway, but Chino's car was also there, so I assumed we had a visitor. I got out, walked up the brick steps, and let myself in.

"Chino!" I called out.

I heard footsteps coming from the formal living room, and I was met with this sexy ass Caramel nigga that made you wanna scream. He was about 6'6", muscular build, and a face made for *Damn, He Fine*. He had a mid length trimmed beard and suckable ass lips. Oh shit, his eyes were honey brown.

"I ain't mean to scare you, ma. I'm True, Chino's cousin from New York," he said in that thick ass New York accent.

"Oh, I forgot he told me you were comin' down. Crazy I'm just meeting you now," I said, still stuck off the sheer sexy, fuck me, fuck me good vibe the nigga had me giving off.

"Yeah, I was in when y'all got together, and then I had moves, so I was chillin' you know? So, I been meeting up with him down here and heading home. You feel me?" He looked me up and down. "But, shorty, I was lookin' for the bathroom." He grabbed his dick, and my stomach tightened at the fact his hand was completely overflowing with dick.

"It's right here around the corner." I pointed and tried to walk fast in the direction he came from to pull myself out his space.

I turned around and saw him watching me as I walked away, so I hurried up turned upon realizing he saw me catch him. I squeezed my eyes tightly and walked into the kitchen were Chino and his other cousin, Medina, whom I did know, were sitting at the breakfast nook.

"Hey, bae." Chino got up and kissed me.

"Wassup cuz." Medina hugged me.

"I'ma introduce you to True when he comes back in here." Chino pulled me onto his lap.

"I met him when I came in. He was lookin' for the bathroom," I said remembering that tense encounter.

"Oh aight, we all about to head out and get some cheese steaks if you wanna roll." He kissed my neck as True came in the kitchen.

Man, the way this nigga locked eyes with me made me wanna push Chino the fuck off.

"No, I think I'll stay," I said, not liking the effect a stranger had on me.

"Nah, come on, shorty. You know I like how you order my shit." Chino scooped me up.

"Put me down, crazy." I giggled and looked at True, who hadn't taken his eyes off me yet.

"Go grab your nigga some money real fast," Chino said.

I went into the closet of our bedroom and took a bundle out the safe then ran back downstairs where they were waiting for me at the door.

We all jumped into Chino's Infiniti and headed out. We always drove a distance because we wanted that authentic shit. Chino and True talked back and forth, and his whole swag had a bitch weak. He had that laid back, Dave East type New York nigga going on, and maaaan.

Once we got the food, we decided to sit in the Great Cheesesteak and eat the shit. I couldn't count how many times me and True locked eyes, but I felt like I was cheating or something.

"So, you still with that one shorty? Fema or whatever?" Chino bursted out.

"Her name was Vee, my nigga. How the fuck you get Fema out of that?" True laughed.

"Ion know, nigga. Weed brain," Chino said.

"But yeah, I still fucks with her. She came with me, but she went to her people spot over in Strawberry Mansion, but she gon' be at Aunt Boot's cook out Saturday," True said.

I knew he had to have him a bitch. There was no way he was single.

I looked towards the door and a large smile adorned my face.

"Aye y'all." Cherry walked in with this dude she fuck with named Tommy.

"Hey, sis, what you doin' here?" I asked and kissed her cheek.

"What you think? Came to get some cheesesteaks." She wrapped her arms around Tommy, being extra for some reason.

"Where Ronnie at?" I asked.

"Wit Iesha," she said, referring to her cousin.

"Oh aight, order your food and sit down," I said to her.

Tommy pulled her along, and they came back to join us. Chino seemed irritated the whole time. I felt like he never really fucked with Cherry like that; he was always this way around her.

I looked up and caught True smiling as he looked at something in his phone. Oh my God, he smiled like a Colgate ad with them perfect teeth.

"Bae," Chino shook me.

"Yeah, nigga, I'm right here," I said, wondering why he was yelling in my damn ear.

"Well, I called you two times. The fuck," he said, balling his food up. "I said is you ready to go?" He looked at me.

True was tuned into me now too.

"Yeah," I said to him.

After saying bye to Cherry and Tommy, we headed back home. I couldn't stop thinking about that mysterious ass nigga True. If he was anything like his cousin, though, he was hell. A fine nigga with a heart of stone.

I SAT in the living room shaking my head at Chino cursing the butch Sandra out. He told her to have an abortion and stopped answering the phone, so she had been calling him from different numbers. He made me sick to my soul with this type of shit. This was his MO. I was disgusted right now.

"I'm sorry, ma. The bitch won't stop calling." Chino hung his phone up.

"Well, it's your fuckin' fault, man. I'm so sick of you." I got up and walked out the living room in my platform peep toes. It was Saturday, and it was time to head to his aunt's cook out.

"Come on, baby. Don't let that bitch fuck us up. You look sexy as fuck, man. I wanna see you happy." He grabbed me up.

"Yeah, well, keep your raggedy dick in your pants and I'll be happy."

I wiggled free and grabbed my purse that contained my

twisted up Ls. I was gon' need them if I was gon' get through today without slapping the shit out of Chino.

"Why my dick gotta be raggedy tho, ma?" he said with this dumb ass look, and I burst out laughing.

"Leave me alone, Chino. Let's just go," I said, ready to walk out the door when he pulled me to him and kissed me slowly.

"I do love you, I swear. Through all my bullshit, you still got my heart, and it never moved. Ever. You my life, ma."

He kissed me again, and I wanted to get excited, but I knew he would devastate my soul again. So, I let him say what he wanted.

I lit up the weed as we drove to his aunt's house in Sharswood. I wasn't about to eat a fucking thing because her house was nasty as fuck, and she picked her nose a lot. Fuck that.

"Let's smoke again real fast," Chino said, lighting up his blunt.

"You don't want them beggin'." I laughed.

"Hell nah, you know they don't ever have no weed." He laughed, and so did I because I knew the reason already.

"There go, True," he said.

When I looked up, I smacked my teeth by accident.

"What's wrong?" Chino asked.

"Nothin', I was gettin' somethin' out my teeth," I lied.

I guess the chick he was walking with was Vee. She was a bad lil bitch or whatever.

"Come here, cuz!" Chino's loud ass called out the window.

True walked up and pulled his bitch with him.

"That shit smells good," he said, taking the blunt I was handing to Chino.

"Damn, nigga," I said, balling my face up.

"Chill," Chino said to me.

"She good. I expect a chick to be mad if a nigga snatch some shit from her. My bad, ma," True said to me.

"Vee, you remember my cousin?" True turned to the girl.

"Yeah, when he came up." She smiled hard as shit.

I looked at a text from Cherry asking where I was, and that she had to talk to me.

Me: Hey, at Chino aunt house for a cook out.

I sent her the vomit emojies.

Bessssfriend: Oh aight, send me the address.

Damn, it must have been important.

I sent it, and we all went inside. I was surprised Aunt Boots cleaned this shit up for the occasion.

"Hey, beautiful girl." Aunt Boots walked up.

"Hey." I smiled and hugged her.

"All the food out back, and Chino, your father over there drunk as hell startin' shit with ya momma," she said.

"Always." Chino shook his head.

I grabbed a cola and went out back to smoke again. A lot of Chino's cousins were out there. As soon as I lit up, they tried to gravitate, but I wasn't having it.

"There go my daughter in law." Chino's mother, Abbie, walked up.

"Hi." I smiled and hugged her.

His father, Brandon, walked up and pushed his mother out the way.

"See, I remember when you used to look like this here." He licked his lips as he looked at me.

"And I remember when your balls used to be under your dick. Now they between your ass cheeks." Abbie smacked the beer out his hand.

"See, bitch." He jumped in her face, and my phone rang just in time

"Hey, sis," I said, seeing it was Cherry.

"I'm here," she said with a shaky voice.

"What's wrong?" I asked before bumping into Medina and dropping my phone.

"Hey boo, we boutta hit this crucial, bitch. Come on." She tried to pull me.

"I'm good, sis." I picked up my phone and saw it was hung up.

I went to the front and didn't see her ass nowhere, so I tried to call her phone again, but it kept going to voicemail. I went out front again and saw that her car was at the end of the block. I walked down, and she wasn't in it. When I walked back and went to the side of the house, I saw her talking to Chino.

"I was just looking for you," I told her.

"Yeah, I was just asking Chino where you were. Look,

I'm feeling sick. I don't know why I just wanted to get out the house." She smiled, but it looked like something was wrong to me.

"Okay, well call me." I hugged her.

"Okay." She started out the door.

Chino and I went back outside, and then his ass disappeared again and left me with True's sexy ass and his girl. We talked a little about shows and shit, but after thirty minutes, I had to go find Chino's simple ass.

I walked everywhere and even went back out front. When I looked the down the block and saw that Cherry's car was still there, for some reason, I got sick. I went into the house and looked up stairs and then went to the backyard and looked around. The basement door was slightly opened, so I went down there.

"Shit," I heard a female faintly say.

"I love you, Chino," I heard, and I knew I must have been lunching.

I ran through the backyard, stomping and moving anybody in my way. I kicked the basement door in and saw Cherry bent over the washing machine with Chino behind her.

"No, no, baby, listen." Chino tried to approach me with his dick swinging.

I pulled my blade and swung it, catching his chest.

"I was coming to tell you, sis," Cherry said and moved when I swung the blade.

"My best friend, Chino!" I screamed.

"Ronnie his son too. I'm tired of hiding my son, Chino," Cherry blurted out.

I covered my mouth, and the tears fell from my eyes on their own.

"That's some fucked up shit, Chino," I heard behind me.

Half the guests stood at the door to witness my embarrassment.

"Let me talk to you." Chino pulled his pants up, and I started laughing.

"I need you to hear this, Chino. We done. I don't give a fuck if that leaves me broke and in a homeless shelter. Just know I won't ever need your trifling ass again. Oh, and you. Community dick, huh?" I looked at Cherry. "Just know every time I see that ass, its mine," I said then pushed my way through the crowd of onlookers and ran through the yard and down the alley.

I was crying so hard my eyes were clouding. A loud horn blared behind me, and I turned in time to see a large truck about to hit me when I was snatched back.

"You almost got hit, ma." I looked up and saw that True was the one who had just saved my life.

"I didn't see it." I sniffled and turned for him to let me down.

I wasn't shit but 5'5", so most niggas were able to pick me up.

"That shit was fucked up. You need a ride somewhere?" he asked with his hand shoved in his jogger jeans.

"Nah, I'm good," I said, not wanting to be around anybody in Chino's bloodline.

"You got some money to get you a room or somethin'?" he said, going into his pockets.

"I'm good."

I walked away from him and hit the corner with some business to handle. I always bust Chino's shit, so I was ready for new blood; Cherry's shit. After looking around, I picked up a loose brick off a vacant stair and went straight to work. I took my blade and cut bitch in the hood and slashed all the tires.

When I saw a crowd coming out front, I went to the bus stop and jumped on the first bus that came. I didn't care to where. I passed his aunt's house and saw Chino and Cherry out front fighting and shit. That tickled me. A lady on the bus looked at me like I was crazy.

I looked in my phone and went to my contact that read Mary. That was my mother. I called, and she picked up on the second ring.

"Hey, Ma," I said as my voice cracked.

"What's wrong?" she asked.

"I need to come home," I cried.

TRUE LUVHER

*T*hat shit was foul as fuck that Chino had going on. It wasn't my business, though, and I know it wasn't my place to chase his shorty, but I'm glad I did. She almost got fucked up. Since I met her, I couldn't keep my eyes off her. I mean, just five minutes around her, and I could feel shorty's soul, and shit was real. Chino took an L, and I knew that without even knowing her ass.

I once had a bitch like her. Man, she was my whole life. Gia got shot while she was pregnant with our son, who also died, when niggas tried to rob my house. We were together since I was a young nigga; she had my back, and I had hers. I was gonna ask her to marry me after the delivery, but I never got a chance. That shit broke me, and I was never able to love like that again. They never found out who did the shit either.

"You been distracted since we left the cook out." Vee snapped me out my daze.

"Yeah, I been thinkin', we need to head back home soon," I said, watching her stand in the bathroom mirror.

We were staying at the Hilton, and I for real couldn't wait to roll. I just needed to come and collect this money from Chino. I was his connect, and I always picked up his money myself. The nigga always had issues with other niggas, but if I knew my blood, he was tryna short me, and they called him.

"I swear, tho, it could not have been a bitch like me. That Passion chick should have cut him some more." She came out and flopped on the bed next to me.

"Mind your business." I kissed her.

"Boy, anyway. So, you know I'm going to Miami for that Jamaican thing, I need some money, pleaseeee. I wanted to ask you the other day, but I got scared you was gon' say no," she whined.

"When I ever say no to you? I think you confusin' me with your husband, babes." I looked at her, and she rolled her eyes.

Shorty was married to this simp ass nigga. She called herself tryna get back at me, but now she was stuck with some three inch dick clown.

"Yeah, well, at least he wanted to be with me, nigga." She smacked her teeth and got up from the bed.

"Man, whatever. But, yeah, like I said, be ready to go home on Tuesday morning."

I looked at my phone and saw I had a wire into my business account with M&T. I had just invested in this computer software company with this dude my Aunt Martina put me onto down there. I had been fucking with him for a few months, which was why I met with him while I was down there. He was supposed to be the best, and he damn sure flipped this shit quick.

I called him and walked on the balcony for privacy.

"I take it you got that deposit," William Santina said when he picked up.

"I ain't know it would be like that, dude. I should have been doin' this stock shit," I told him.

"Yeah 700K ain't bad on your first go around. Now, imagine when we do more." He chuckled.

"I hear you, but I'ma be heading home on Tuesday, so I might wanna come talk about some more possibilities," I told him.

I wasn't no dumb nigga. I was gon' flip my money a hundred ways before I was done. Feds won't know where the fuck to look.

"Well, listen, my daughter just came back home, so we're all gonna go to dinner if you wanna join us tomorrow," he offered.

"Aight, that's a bet. Just let me know what time," I said.

"Will do." He hung up.

"Who was dat?" Vee asked and threw her arms around my waist.

"When you start payin' my phone bill, you can ask me

some shit like that." I kissed her and pushed her back on the bed.

"I know you don—" I covered her mouth with my lips to shut her the fuck up and pulled down her underwear from under her teddy.

"Helicopter on this dick." I laid on my back, and she got into this position he always did that drove me the fuck crazy.

After sliding down on my dick, she pulled both her feet behind her head and held her arms out, then I spun her around. It was like I was getting head and my dick beat at the same time. I ain't never seen a bitch do no wild shit like that.

I got ready to cum, but I didn't want to yet, so I pulled her up and put her in a wheel barrel.

"Oh my God, True, you crazy," she said as her voice cracked up from me pounding into her.

I bit down on my bottom lip and zoned out in that pussy. The way she moaned was sexier than fuck, and it always made me wanna buss.

"Fuck." I pulled out even though I had a condom on.

"Damn, daddy," she cooed as I let her legs down.

She swung up and jumped on me, kissing on my neck. I lay back on the bed as she still straddled me. Her phone started ringing, and she jumped up to answer it. I knew it was her corny ass husband.

"Hey." She ran into the bathroom and closed the door.

I chuckled and took my phone off the nightstand. I saw that Chino had hit me.

Chino: *I need your help cuz*

Me: *What nigga*

I ain't come down here to do no favors and shit, man. This nigga kept some shit going, so I knew it was fuck shit already.

Chino: *Come thru the crib for me.*

I exhaled deeply and got up to shower. I always made sure to be fresh when I left to go anywhere.

"Why you gotta leave? We just getting back," Vee whined.

"Shut your ass up. You ain't my girl, ma, stop questionin' me." I got dressed and brushed my hair.

"Yeah, well, you had the chance to make that shit happen, muthafucka. Fuck you, matta fact." She got up and went in the bathroom then slammed the door.

I ain't pay her ass no type of attention because she would jump on a nigga when I got back. Spoiled ass.

"Be back," I said loud enough for her to hear me and went out the door.

I headed to Chino's spot, and for some reason, my mind wandered to shorty's lil ass. I licked my lips thinking about her. I wasn't no grimy nigga, so I wouldn't dare step on my cousin's toes, but damn. I turned my music up, drowned out my own thoughts, and went to see what this dumb nigga had goin' on.

Once I pulled up to the house, I saw Chino outside pacing and shit. I jumped out, and he ran up to me.

"Nigga, I fucked up," he said.

"The fuck happened, nigga?" I asked.

"I killed her. That bitch, Sandra, came here talkin' 'bout callin' the feds on a nigga," he said as he walked into the house with me following.

I was able to see her body from the door. As I approached, I saw she had a hole in her forehead.

"Nigga, why you ain't call a clean up crew?" I asked.

"Cuz, the nigga I was usin' got locked up. I figured you could help me with somebody," he said.

"Nigga." I pulled out my phone and send a text to the homie down here. Relentless clean up. That's what Dookey called his business.

"Nigga, do betta," I said.

"Man, the bitch told me she wanted to suck my dick, so of course I let her come thru. Then she started all that be with her shit, and then said she would hit the feds, and I snapped. Shit is her fault," he said and kicked her leg.

"You just lost your shorty, and you still doin' fuck, shit," I said in disgust.

"Nigga, why you worried about me and my bitch? She comin' right back like she always do. She said it's over, so I'm single until then." He laughed.

I ain't share in his laughter. I went to the mini bar and got a drink while I waited for Dookey to show up and do his job.

I had a text from my mother saying she loved me and would see me when I got back. She was always worried about me and always sent shit like that. Her and my father were like night and day. He was locked up when I was born and got out when I was seven. My mother grew up poor but decided she wanted better, so she went to college and became a nurse. My father was a hustla, and they met at the courthouse. He swept her off her feet, but then he got killed.

She used to tell me that he said women wasn't shit but pussy and cooks. If that was the case, I ain't never think like him, but I do love multiple bitches. That's why I don't ever call myself taken. Ain't no point in hurting them for no reason when I could just be free.

"That nigga here," Chino said, looking out the window.

"Aight, I'm boutta bounce. That nigga charge 20K, so I hope you got it," I told him.

"Man, twenty, what the fuck." He shook his head.

"The nigga ain't just takin' out your trash cuz you got a fuckin' first degree murder charge on your floor of a pregnant bitch at that."

I left and headed back to the room. Just like I thought, Vee's ass was waiting and ready for another round, and I put her ass to sleep and went right along with her.

"I hope I'm dressed right," Vee said, fidgeting with her clothes again.

We had to come to Mr Santina's house because he said his daughter didn't feel like going out.

"You look good. Chill," I said because she was doing too damn much.

The door opened and a pretty ass older lady smiled at us.

"Hey, you must be True, and—" She reached her hand out in Vee's direction.

"I'm Velencia, but everybody calls me, Vee." She shook her hand.

"Well, William is waiting for you," she said as she let us in.

I looked around the house and the shit was dope, looked like my house in New York. Well one of them, I had a few.

We followed her to the dining room where the table was set up. The food looked good as hell. Fried chicken was my favorite, so when I saw it, I was ready. There was a white guy and a chick who looked like a young Mary sitting there with him.

"Hey, I just got Chauncey to pour you a drink for dinner." Mr. Santina got up and shook my hand and then kissed Vee's. "This is our daughter, Alexandria, and her husband, Mark." Mr. Santina introduced us.

"Hi." She smiled and went back into her phone.

"Hey, buddy." Mark waved.

"How y'all doin'," I said as I sat down.

"Glad to have you here," Mary said.

"Thanks. Looks good," I said, looking to Mary in case she cooked.

"Thanks, we got it catered from a place we own downtown," Mary responded. "I don't know why my daughter is insisting on being difficult." Mary got up and walked out but came back shortly after.

"True, this is our daughter, Passion." Mary sat down and Passion walked in.

"True, what you doin' here?" Passion asked.

"You two know each other?" Mary asked.

"Yeah, he's Chino's cousin," Passion said.

"You related to that degenerate," Alexandria said.

"Well, you're certainly cut from a different cloth," Mr Santina said.

"My cousin doesn't need to be brought up," I said, looking at Passion.

"Alright, well, let's eat," Mary said as Passion sat down.

"So, what do you plan to do once you make the money I think you can?" Mr Santina asked me.

"I don't know, Mr. S—"

"Call me William," he interjected.

"I don't know, William, I think I can open a few businesses. I'm interested in a few things right now," I told him.

"That's good. I'm glad you have a plan. I can get you one of the business managers in New York," he said.

"Can you wait to talk business later? Alex said she had news," Mary said.

"Yes. So, as you know, we been trying for a baby, and

guess what?" Alex pulled out a ziplock bag that contained a pregnancy test.

"Oh my God!" Mary screamed.

"Finally, a grand child," William said.

"Congrats," Passion said then got up and walked out.

"I don't know what is wrong with her." Alex shook her head. We continued to eat, and I had to piss after two drinks.

"Can I use the bathroom?" I asked, standing up.

"Yeah, its right down the hall," William said.

I got up and went down the hall, passing a set of French doors where I heard crying. I was a nosey nigga, so I opened them and went out to a large rose garden and saw Passion crying at a white iron table.

"You aight, ma?" I asked, startling her.

She wiped her eyes quickly, and I sat down with her.

"I'm good. Why didn't you tell me you knew my father?" she asked.

"I didn't know he was your pops. But you gon' tell me what you feelin' right now?" I asked at her.

"Well, you already know why I'm hurtin', so why say it?" She looked at me with those red, puffy eyes.

"You don't seem like the rest of your family," I said, changing the subject.

"And what are they like?" she turned to me, and she had nothing but anger dripping from her voice.

"Shorty, you mad at the wrong nigga. Calm the fuck

down, I don't like that shit," I said not liking how she was comin' at a nigga.

"Well, excuse me for not bein' in the best mood, my nigga." She cut her eyes at me.

"You got some gas? Maybe you need to smoke." I clamped my hands.

"I ain't got none." She leaned back.

"Come on. Lemme use the bathroom, and I got you," I told her and stood up.

"Okay." She jumped up with me.

After I used the bathroom, we went to my car. I rolled up a spliff and gave her the rest of the bag. She was about to get out my whip when I sparked up.

"Stay." I handed her the weed, and she accepted.

She smelled good as hell too. If she wasn't Chino's shorty, I would have been up in her guts.

"Your cousin' a fuckin' clown," she said out of nowhere.

"That shit ain't got nun to do wit me. That's y'all thing," I said.

"So, why the fuck you actin' like I could talk to you then? Ugh, you know what. Here," she said, trying to hand the spliff back.

"I don't know what you used to, but you ain't gon' keep snappin' on me. Pipe your ass down, no bullshit." I frowned at her.

She looked like she couldn't believe I came at her like that, but she kept smoking.

"I wasn't tryna seem like I ain't care, but I know how this

shit go. Some females go right back, and I don't wanna hear it if that's the case," I said.

"Well, don't worry, I ain't. Shit, I was thinkin' about coming up to New York to start over. Maybe Coney Island or somethin'," she said.

"That would be dope. What you plan on doin' out there?" I asked.

"I got a CNA certificate. I might try to be a full nurse." She shrugged.

"You could be a good one, I'm sure. Saving lives and shit, that's what's up, ma." I nodded at her in admiration.

"Thanks." She blushed.

Passion was a real cute joint. One of them shorties you can just look at.

"Well, maybe when you come up, I can—"

"This where the hell you went?" I heard Vee's muffled voice through the window.

"My bad, I was smokin'," I told her.

"Your father lookin' for you," Vee said, looking Passion up and down like she thought we were up to something.

"Thanks. And thanks, True." Passion got out and walked toward the house.

Vee had come out and fucked shit up. We were kind of vibing.

"You know that rich nigga ain't about to let you near his daughter," Vee said.

"Shut your jealous ass up." I got out and sprayed on some Gucci cologne.

"Whatever. Can you let me know when we leaving? That girl Alexandria is annoying as fuck." She smacked her teeth.

"In a lil bit. Let me holla at William," I told her as we walked back in.

Me and William sat in the den drinking more brandy while the girls had dessert.

"So, what do you do? Clearly whatever it is brings you money to invest large sums," he said.

"A little of everything."

"I figured you would say something like that. That's why I covered for you on your paperwork. I have dealt with a lot of drug dealers and made them even richer."

"What you mean?" I asked like I didn't know what the fuck he was talking about.

"You ever heard of a man named Guy?" he asked me.

That was my plug. How the fuck this nigga know names? I never met Guy because his right hand, Ace, said he didn't want shit to be traced to him.

"You a fed or some shit, nigga?" I asked, sitting forward.

He ain't even sound the same as when I got there. He was trying to feel a nigga out with that fake white guy bullshit.

"No, I'm Guy," he said.

"What?" I stood up.

"Chill," he said calmly.

"What's all this shit, man? Feels like a setup." I squinted.

"Ain't no setup, nigga. Your aunt knows who the fuck I

am. Ask her," he barked. This nigga's tone changed like a motherfucker.

"So, why the game?" I asked.

"It wasn't a game. I'm a investor. I invest in my people." He threw an envelope on the table.

I picked it up took out a black card.

"The hell is this shit?" I, asked flipping it over and seeing my name.

"That's your key to the streets, nigga. Whenever you get a text to your phone, follow the directions there, and that opens all doors," he said.

"This shit sound crazy," I said, looking at the card.

"It is. I also wanna set up another person in New York. They won't step on your toes, but they'll work next to you."

"Who?" I asked, because regardless of who he was, I was New York, and I ain't need niggas steppin' on my toes for shit because then it would be a problem.

"I don't know yet. I'll let you know," he said. "Oh, and tell your cousin the only reason I didn't step to him was because of my daughter. He needs to stay away from her, you feel me?" he said, getting up and extending his hand.

I nodded and shook it. I wasn't about to let nobody harm my blood, so I didn't give a fuck what that shit meant.

I left with Vee confused as hell. This damn sure wasn't what I was expecting when I agreed to dinner. I felt the card that I was handed and got curious as hell, so I called my aunt, and she explained it all. She was Mary's best friend back in the day, and they still kept close. I was gon' find out about all that shit.

Why did he agree to reveal himself to me? Did Passion know her father was my connect? I never trusted nobody and never believed in coincidences. But that's why I kept one eye open.

I MOVED my bed across the floor and opened the hatch to the false floor. After I grabbed my .45 and a bundle, I closed it back up. I ran downstairs where Lucci was sitting on the couch with one of the chicks who came to the lil gathering I was having. It was bitches everywhere, and it was live as fuck.

This was a loft I had for shit like this. Sometimes I ain't feel like driving home from this side, so I stayed there. I had a 5 bedroom brownstone in Tribeca. I loved that shit too; I lived by celebrities and shit. I keep hoping Rihanna's fine ass would move next door because I would demolish that pussy.

"Aye, nigga, we ready to start the show. We boutta make it rain on these hoes." Lucci pulled out a bundle.

Me and Lucci had been cool for a little over ten years. I saw the nigga like a brother. We did a lot of dirt together and came up on this money together too. He handled the fire arms and shit, and I moved weight like Dr. Nazario.

"Turn the stage on," I told Beast, who stood by the stripper stage in the loft.

Music started, and the first broad took the stage. She was fine as fuck, too. I had already decided she was the one I was fuckin' on tonight. She had that long ass ponytail that tapped her thick ass.

"Shit. Bitch got a nigga ready." I chuckled.

"Yeah, she a nice piece, but I'm waitin' for that red bitch over there." He pointed.

"Dag, nigga." The chick who sat next to him got up.

I laughed, and he looked dumbfounded.

"Forgot her ass was there." Lucci shrugged.

"So, did that nigga, Guy, send somebody out here?" he asked.

"He supposed to be sending somebody tonight. I been waiting, but he ain't tell me who yet. Shit wild to me, though. That shit yesterday was even wilder."

I shook my head, thinking about when I showed up with that black card at a location I was texted. The shit was some type of Luxury ass drug warehouse. Keys a mile long, weed, pills, acid. Everything you needed. Shit, I guess that's why he called it the key to the streets. They even had guns and shit, but I got my own heat. I ain't need them for that.

"Yeah, real talk. Shit, we need to get like that too, blood." He looked at me.

"Shit, nigga we ain't hurtin' out here," I said while watching the shorty finish her routine.

"I already know that, nigga."

"So, what you sayin'?" I looked at him. "Nigga, we can be our own plug, nigga. Shit, one day."

"Yeah, one day," he said and directed his eyes to the stage when the chick he was talking about hit the pole.

"What's your name, lil ma?" I grabbed the chick who just left the stage.

"Vixen." She giggled.

"Nah, I mean your real name, ma." I smirked.

"Laru." She shifted her weight to one side and cocked her head.

"That's cool. Look, won't you go get cleaned up and come holla at me, aight?" I winked.

She smiled and walked to the back where I told them they could dress.

My phone started vibrating, and I saw a text from a blocked number.

Private: *Call this number for your next door neighbor. 2156720000*

I looked at the text sideways and wondered if it was Guy. I ain't bother to deal with the shit tonight.

"New Freezer don't give a fuck!" one of my niggas yelled.

"True shit! We never give a fuck. Get this money and fuck shit else!" I said, standing up with my bottle. "We run shit, and every mufucka who set foot on that concrete knows that. We take no prisoners and never surrender. New freezer!" I turned my bottle up.

"Ayyyyee!!" they all cheered.

These were my niggas, the New Freezer Boys. Me and

Lucci started calling ourselves that when we began to get iced out and shit. It picked up when we started our own crew and shit, so that's what we were.

"So, what's up?" The chick, Laru, came back and sat down.

"Me and you up in that bedroom like now." I looked at her seriously.

"Damn, you move fast." She blushed.

"I do. I use my own condoms, so don't even think you boutta trap a nigga." I chuckled but was dead ass serious.

"Boy, I ain't about to let no baby fuck up this body, honey." She smirked.

I took her upstairs and blew her back the fuck out. She was calling a nigga daddy before the night was over. I ain't no bragging nigga, but I got that eleven inch monster for these bitches. I was blessed as fuck down there, and I used that shit to murder pussy.

After I bust my nut and kicked her out the room, I picked up the phone and decided to call the number Guy sent.

"Hey, this is Passion. You missed me, hit a bitch back."

I heard Chino shorty's voice on the other end. This nigga sent his fuckin' daughter to New York. What the fuck? Chino ain't tell me she was in the streets. Niggas would eat chicks up out here, and I ain't wanna see her fucked up tryna play this game. I hung up the phone and decided to hit her again in a few days. I had to think about this shit.

CHINO

"You brought all that dumb shit on yourself. Stupid bitch." I looked at Cherry crying on the bed with a face full of fresh bruises.

I hated this bitch right now, and her tears and plea's meant shit to me.

"I fuckin' hate you!" she screamed.

I turned to her. "I hate you too, bitch, that's why you never meant shit. You ain't shit like Passion, that's why you ain't no wifey type bitch to me. A quick nut and an aight cook is all you is. So, next time you think about playin' fuck games with me, remember you ain't shit." I threw the TV, and it crashed in the corner.

"Good, so now I know that. All you worry about is your son, bitch." She tried to hit me, and I grabbed her arms and pushed her back on the bed.

"That's all I ever worried about. That's why he at Ma's

51

house, so I can whoop your ass in peace." I slapped the shit out her, and she rolled off the bed.

"Why the fuck you had to come do that shit to her? She ain't been shit but a good friend to your sorry ass."

"You really one crazy ass nigga. She your woman, and you asked why I do that to her."

"Philadelphia PD," I heard a loud voice boom in the living room.

"Bitch, you called the police!" I said then ran to the bathroom and leapt out the window.

I ran down the alley and kept running for a few minutes until I felt that I was a safe distance away.

"My fuckin' car," I said aloud and out of breath.

I took out my phone and called Lox.

"What's good?" he said when he picked up.

"Nigga, I need you to scoop a nigga up, man. That bitch, Cherry, wild," I said, walking into the corner store.

"Damn, nigga, you always got some bullshit goin' on."

"Nigga, I done rescued yo ass before, so return the favor," I said, catching an attitude. "Lemme get some Capones." I pulled a twenty out and grabbed a pack of gum.

"Where you at?" he asked.

"At the corner store three blocks down from her house. That lil red joint, just go straight," I told him and hung up.

I was walking out when two Spanish bitches were walking in. The one on the right was cuter and thicker, so I went there.

"Hola mami. I mean, damn," I said, looking at her ass as she walked by.

"I got a boyfriend." She smiled.

"So, I wanna be ya friend." I touched her hair, and she blushed.

"Come on, Christa," the shorty with her said.

"Christa, huh?" I licked my lips, and she pushed her hair behind her ear.

Her buddy stomped off.

"Lemme call you. Just let a nigga know when your dude around, aight ma?" I handed her my phone, and she put her number in.

"I'ma wait outside because you takin' forever," her friend said and walked out.

"I don't know what her problem is." Christa shook her head.

"I ain't trippin' I'ma hit you, okay?" I walked out and saw the other chick in her phone.

"Why you so mad?" I asked her.

"Mad about what?" she said and turned up her lip.

"What's your name?" I asked.

"Misandra, why?" she said with an attitude.

"You wanted me to holla at chu, huh?" I smirked.

"Nah, I'm cool, papi." She tried to walk by.

"You wet right now. Stop fuckin' playin' wit me and gimme your number," I told her in her ear.

She started to breath heavily, and I knew I was right.

Just as Lox pulled up, she quickly gave me her number. I jumped in, and he checked her out before we pulled off.

"Nigga, you got bitch problems already, and you can't stop, huh?" He looked at me and laughed.

"Shit, I got her and her friend's number. I'll pass them hoes to y'all when I'm done."

"Nigga, you know I don't fuck behind your ass." He looked at his phone and quickly put it to his ear.

"Yeah, yeah, I got him wit' me," he said.

"Don't be tellin' niggas I'm here, bruh." I looked at his ass.

"It's Shakey, nigga," Lox told me.

"Oh, aight."

"He say we need to meet him at the trap. Some niggas came askin' about a chick name Sandra. Said she was last with you or some shit." Lox looked at me.

"Nah, bitch wasn't wit me," I lied.

I ain't mean to kill Sandra, but I was already hot with Cherry, and then that bitch came yapping and pissed me off.

Lox hung up, and that shit ain't move me about her people coming at me.

My cell now rang, and it was Cherry's stupid ass.

"I ain't call the police," she said as soon as I picked up.

"I don't even give a fuck, shorty. We done, man. If it ain't about Ronnie, don't fuckin' call me." I hung up.

That shit made me wanna call Passion's ass to see if it

was time for me to work my magic and get her back home. The phone rang and rang then went to voicemail.

"Aye, baby, can you at least call a nigga back, tho?" I left a voicemail and hung up.

"Passion still duckin'?" Lox asked.

"Yeah, but she needs to get her shit together, man."

"What you expect, tho? You got her best friend pregnant and let her be on dumb for three years," Lox said.

"Whatever, man. I ain't mean that shit. I love my girl, man," I said.

Looking out the window, I thought about when I first met bae.

I WAS NAVIGATING my way through people at my cousin Gucci's party in the basement of my aunt's house. Music blasted through the speakers, and everybody was dancing, smoking, and getting fucked up. The bitch Esha that I came with was irritating my whole soul, and I just wanted her to shut the fuck up. I had a bet, though, and I wasn't about to lose money. So, I went into action to duck the bitch.

"I mean, she could have at least had more chairs," she complained.

I looked past her at this girl who was dancing, having fun and shit. She was cute as hell, and I liked how she looked in that skirt and halter. She locked eyes with me, and that shit made my dick hard.

"Let's go in the room," I said to Esha and rubbed on her perfect, round ass.

"You nasty." She giggled and got off the couch.

The whole night, she had been complaining about everything, and now I just wanted to put my dick in her mouth to shut her up. She was supposed to have the best head on the block, and my homie bet me I couldn't get the shit.

"Right here is good." I kissed her neck and pulled her into my cousin's room, separate from the basement living space.

"It's cute in here," she said, looking at the nice décor my cousin had going on. He did this shit just for bitches to be impressed.

"You got some pretty ass lips," I said and pulled my dick out.

"Oh, uh uh. Why you can't give me head first?" she said, looking down.

"Bitch, fuck you talkin' 'bout first? I ain't eatin' your pussy. Fuck told you that? Bitch, I know you had more dicks than a right hand." I put my dick back up.

"Oh nah, oh nah. Take me the fuck home, nigga. I ain't come out here to be disrespected." She flipped her hair.

"Call a cab." I stomped out the room and realized I had lost out on one hundred and fifty dollars.

"Oh, I'm sorry."

I felt somebody bump into me. The perfume hit me first, and that shit made my dick jump back up. I saw the prettiest, slanted eyed, prefect faced, angel bitch standing in front of me.

"Hey, shorty. What's good?" I boldly wrapped my arms around her waist.

She laughed and almost fell back. I could tell she was drunk.

"I'm Passion. You cute." She smiled.

"That's a pretty name, ma. I'm Chino." I looked her in the eyes.

"Alex, this is Chino," she said to a girl who had her nose turned up.

"Hi. Are you ready to go now?" Alex looked at me then Passion.

"Ugh, you always wanna run back home. The fuck," Passion said angrily.

"Fine, catch a damn bus." The chick Alex stomped out.

"That's your friend?" I asked her.

"No, my sister." She looked in the direction Alex left in. "I'ma have to catch up to her. I can't be catching no bus from here alone. I live far," she said.

"I can give you a ride," I told her.

"Oh, no the fuck you didn't. Nigga, I came here with your ass, and you told me to catch a damn cab." Esha came up to me.

"Yeah, bitch, I wanted my dick sucked, and you said no. So, I'm offering shorty a chance to go on dates and shit, spend money, and be my lil bitch if she wants without even seeing my dick, and Ion even know her," I said looking at Passion, who looked intrigued by what I said.

"This bitch ain't shit," Esha said, trying to pick a fight.

"She bad as a mufucka. I know that shit." I grabbed Passion's hand and walked her out the basement door.

"You need a ride?" I asked.

"Yeah, but I'm hungry as hell." She rubbed her stomach.

"Let's get some food then." I felt like I just wanted to be around her.

We went to this steak joint down by the bell. I only had three hundred on me, and since I didn't want the night to end, I hit up Lox like I always did when I was in a jam. He had been my homie since the sandbox, so he brought me a stack.

"You wanna go to the movies?" I asked Passion.

"Why you being so nice to me?" she asked suspiciously

"Because I like you," I spoke honestly.

"You don't even know me." She laughed.

"I want to, tho." I pulled her to me and slowly kissed her. That shit felt so good.

I met her two hours ago, and she already had me hooked.

We went to the movies and barely saw the screen as we tongued each other down. I wanted to fuck her bad as shit, but it was something about her that made me wanna take shit slow. When I went to drop her off, I pretty much figured she lived like this. She wasn't a hood chick, and it was written on her whole demeanor. Before she got out, I need one more.

"You gotta promise to call me or I ain't lettin' you out." I kissed her.

"You already know I'm callin'." She smiled and kissed me.

"Aight, ma." I watched her walk up to the large wood doors.

That was how I got my shorty, and I had been fucking up ever since. I called Passion and left another voicemail. I felt a real loss, and I couldn't take the shit. I needed her to come home.

I saw a text from Cherry and shook my head. I had saved

her name in my phone under a dude's name because her dumb ass sometimes tried to call when she knew I was with Passion.

Carlos: Can you come back? I'm sorry.

Me: Hell no. Fuck you

I changed her name in my phone.

Passionwannabe: Let's talk. I just wanted to get the shit out there, Chino. It wasn't fair to Ronnie.

I locked my phone and ignored her ass. She always wanted to use our son as a reason for her bullshit. Fuck that bitch. I was gon' get Passion back and marry her quick.

PASSION

I sat on the bed and thought about the conversation I heard my father and True having that night. My father was a drug dealer; that shit was crazy to me. I always felt like he was a little off in ways, and now I knew why. He needed to know that I knew, though. I walked downstairs and saw him sitting in the den looking over some papers.

"Dad." I walked in, and he looked up.

"Hey, baby girl." He sat back and yawned.

"I wanna be the one you send up to New York," I blurted out.

"What?" he looked like he had seen a ghost.

"I heard you the other night. I know everything. I've seen Chino for years, and I think I can do it," I said, not allowing him to get over the initial shock of me finding out who he was.

"I would never send my daughter to be no fuckin' connect." His tone had turned real gangsta.

"I don't have shit goin' on. I know I can do the shit. Just cuz I'm a female don't mean I can't handle my shit. You see, I ain't shit like Alex. I know the streets, and I wanna do it. If not, I'll start my own thing," I said.

"Are you fuckin' kidding me? Why don't you do the nurse thing?" he said.

"No, I wanna do this. I can be a boss bitch," I said adamantly.

"You serious about this shit?" he asked.

"And why can't she? How you meet me, Guy?" my said when she walked in.

"Wait, Ma, you know about this?" I asked.

"Duh, who you think put him on? I was the dope queen by the time I was twenty-three then your father came along and wanted me to be his wife, so I let him lead," she said, surprising the fuck out of me.

How the fuck didn't I know this about my family?

"It's funny. I always told your father no matter how we tried to shelter you from that hood shit, it was born in you. I think you can do the shit," my mother said to me.

"I never wanted them in the game. You know that," my father said.

"Yeah, well it seems like she gon' do it with or without you, so wouldn't you rather be on the inside?" She cocked her head.

"We can talk about this shit later." He breathed heavily.

"Well, I wanna be gone by next week." I got up.

"Aight, you know what? If you think you got it, cool. If you fuck up one time, I'm throwing somebody else on it. I don't play no games, not even with my fuckin' daughter. Go pack, you leaving in a few days," he said, looking in his phone as my mother smirked.

"Can I ask you something?" I looked at my mother as she helped get my clothes together.

"Yes?" She raised her eyebrow.

"Why y'all didn't just keep shit one hundred. My whole life I felt some shit was wrong with me, but I realize it's in my blood. Alex a stuck up white bitch and some more shit." I shook my head.

"Because we wanted better for y'all. But I can see so much of me in you. Focus on the money, Passion. You hear me?" She hugged me and walked out.

I don't know what snapped in me that made me wanna do some shit like this, but I could be a boss. I would never be some weak lil' bitch ever again.

"This dope, Ma," I told my mother.

I was in my 17th floor penthouse on the upper east side. I just got there, and I was already in love. I had heard Chino's messages on the drive up, and I blocked his ass. I didn't wanna hear the shit. This was a new me, and I was never going back to Chino; I didn't care what he said. I was officially done.

"I knew you would like it. It was mine. I got an indoor pool built here." She pointed through the double doors. "And the kitchen, oh my God." She smiled.

"I didn't know you lived in New York," I said.

"Yeah, for years. I always loved it here." She looked out at the view.

"I wish daddy would have come. He just gave me this." I pulled out the black card.

"The key to the streets." She smiled.

"That's what he said. What does that mean?" I asked.

"It's something I made up. Did he give you the phone?" she asked.

"Yeah." I pulled it out.

"Addresses will come and you go. Simple." She hugged me. "I gotta run, I wanna go see some people. Oh, and your cousin Pashia on the way over." She turned and pointed.

"Oh okay, cool." I nodded.

Pashia was her sister's daughter. She was cool as shit, and she was already in the streets. She was a pretty ass gangsta; she had no time for games and played none.

I waited for her to arrive and thought about the responsibility I was taking on. I felt brave, so fuck it. I was gon' Queen this motherfucker.

The elevator sounded, and I looked at the large monitor and saw it was Prashia. I put in the code to let her in, and she screamed when she saw me.

"Man, I couldn't wait until you got here. I been talking to aunt Mary and shit. So, what you doin' out here? School?" she asked then burst out laughing. "I'm fuckin wit chu. I see they finally let y'all in on shit," she said.

"Not y'all, me. Alex would probably call the police." I giggled.

"My mother used to say y'all had to be blind. But fuck all that, you need some help runnin' shit? I mean, I freelance, but if you need some slots filled, my whole crew is lit, blood. All bitches too," she said proudly.

"Shit, well let me talk to them," I said.

"I'll set it up. Let's smoke some shit up, tho." She rolled up.

"So, you got a dude or somethin'," she asked, blowing out her smoke.

"Nah, I had one. Nigga played me somthin' serious." I scoffed.

"Don't they tend to do that? I finally got a good one, though, so I'm straight." She shrugged.

"That's wassup, Pashia," I said, happy for her.

"Oh, I gotta have you out here in these streets, so we need to head out one night. Soon, like this weekend soon," she demanded.

"Aight, that's a bet. Let's do the damn thang," I said as I slow bounced.

I FELT SO happy to be with my family up there because I never really got to see them. I was dressed down and ready to head out with Pashia and two girls from her crew, Dela and Fatima. She said they were close to her, more like sisters. Dela looked like a chocolate Barbie. I swear she don't look like a hitta, but that's what Pashia was giving her praises and shit for. Fatima looked like she was off. She had this cut on her eye that gave her character, and she was extremely skinny and quiet except when spoken to.

When my mother's sister, Zalaine, heard me and Pashia were going out, she insisted we stop there first. She had called the whole New York family over. I felt uncomfortable dressed like a skank around all my people.

"We need to hurry up," Pashia said in my ear.

"Aight cool," I said then walked to my aunt and kissed her cheek.

"Y'all tryna run out of here to be nasty," Aunt Zalaine said.

"You know that's what it is," my cousin, Darnell, said, looking at me strangely. That shit made me feel uncomfortable, to be honest.

"I'll come back. It's warm, so we can do a cook out or something." I kissed my aunt and said bye to my cousins.

"Girl, you know she ain't never gon' leave you alone now," Pashia said, walking ahead of me.

"Damn, that ass tho, cuz."

I looked at her body, and she was set. My body wasn't

bad, but I ain't have no huge bubble ass. It was cute or whatever.

"Let's hit that lil spot on 175th sis. They got some fine ass money in there. That's how I met my last two exes." Dela laughed.

"Girl, no, this joint Daddy in Harlem, honey, that's the spot," Pashia retorted.

"Oh, nah, I heard them some sweet boys. Let's do Brooklyn. It's plenty of spots." Dela shrugged.

"Right. That's coo too. Plus, my bae, Lucci, be up there." Pashia stuck her tongue out.

"Who is Lucci?" I asked.

"My bae, one of them. He be with them New Freezer niggas." She smiled.

"Oh, well look, let's get goin'. I'm ready to drink up," I said.

"Oh look, he said his mans doin' a lil party at his spot. Let's check it out, I wanna see my lil boo." Pashia popped her lips.

"Hell yeah, I mean of course we got bread, but it's free," Fatima said. She had on a cute outfit, but lord, she still looked like a gargoyle. Poor thing.

"Aight, I'm tellin' him we on the way," Pashia said.

We drove a nice ass distance before we got to these large buildings. I relaxed, they were lofts and condos from the signs.

"I can hear the music already," Dela said, snapping her fingers and shaking her titties.

"Damn, ma. Shake that shit," a fine ass nigga with with slick waves and a diamond shaped ice chain around his neck said.

"Hey daddy, what's good?" Dela smiled in his face.

The dudes he walked with had that same chain on as they passed us and walked inside the building.

"Come on, Dela," Pashia said, but Dela waved us on and walked with the dude into the building.

"Girl, she ain't even scan the scene yet," Pashia said in my ear.

We got on a large elevator and went up. Once the doors opened, it was flashing lights, weed smoke, and ass everywhere.

"Bitch, your nigga in here?"

I looked at all the scattered ass and bitches on stripper poles and shit. The music was bumping, and I couldn't deny it was lit as fuck in there. I felt the vibe and decided to ride this wave and enjoy myself. There was a little make shift bar on the right of the room, so that's where I wanted to be. I always rolled a few spliffs when I stepped out, so I took one out and lit it.

"Let's get a drink," I told Pashia.

"Lemme find Lucci ass real fast." She grabbed my hand and walked through with Fatima right behind us. She looked fascinated by the strippers.

"Dang, this shit on point," she said and accidentally bumped into a stripper.

"My bad, but damn, you gon. have to give me dance."
Fatima eyed the chick.

"Shit, we can do that," the stripper said, and she pulled
Fatima with her.

"She gay?" I asked Pashia.

"Yeah, she bi. She can't get many dudes, but she can get
bitches. I guess females like they cat ate no matter what you
look like." She laughed.

"You petty."

"Ooh, there his ass go. Look at him surrounded by tricks."

Pashia looked over toward this guy who had a female on
both sides. He was cute too, a brown skin average size dude.
I looked to his right and squinted.

"That's True, Chino's cousin," I told her.

"I know who he is, but I ain't know he was Chino's
people. He the head of all this. It's his party. He the dude
who owns New York. You might wanna be nice since you
here on your own business."

True had a pretty ass female sitting in his lap. She was
all smiles and in this nigga's face like she was ready to give
that pussy up now. As fine as he was, I didn't blame her.

"Come on, girl." Pashia walked up and stood in front of
the dude Lucci.

I tried not to look in True's direction, but my eyes
wandered and saw him looking at me.

"Y'all bitches need to step the fuck off." Pashia mugged
on them bitches.

"Baby, stop trippin', you know I'm just talkin'." The dude Lucci grabbed for her, and she smacked his hand away.

"Girl, sit the fuck down. Y'all hoes gotta move," he told the females.

"Who dis?" He looked at me.

"My cousin, Passion."

"Wait, Passion Santina?" he said.

"Nigga, chill," True said, finally breaking his silence.

"And how you know me?" I asked, feeling alarmed.

"Have a seat, ma," True said to me.

The girls who sat with Lucci at first left angrily, and I sat down.

"I like your nails. I be getting mine done at the mall," the chick who sat in his lap said.

"Thanks. I got them done at home."

"You home now. I hear you moved out here." True rubbed the chick's ass.

"I guess. I wouldn't call it home yet."

"Where you from?" Lucci asked me.

"Philly."

"This Chino's girl," True said.

"I ain't Chino's shit, aight. I moved on from his ass," I snapped.

"Calm the fuck down, ma. You say that now," True said.

He was getting on my fucking nerves.

"Man, I'ma bounce," I said to Pashia.

True started laughing. "Damn, all it takes is some words

to hurt your feelins, shorty? How you gon' boss up?" He laughed and got up with the chick.

"I'ma be right back." True looked at me and walked off with the chick.

"He rude as fuck," I said, feeling hot from that look he gave me before he walked off.

"He aight. Look, they got some Moet, bitch." She picked up a bottle out of the ice and grabbed two flutes off the table.

"Make sure them hoes wasn't drinkin' out those, sis." I looked at the glasses.

"They clean, they was turned over, girl." She laughed.

"So, what y'all was getting' into? I mean, I want you to come wit' me when it's over, shorty." Lucci kissed on Pashia.

"Boy, I bet you told them hoes that too, that's why we can't get serious." She rolled her eyes.

"I ain't tell them hoes shit, and we is serious. Stop sayin' that," he said and kissed her.

I rolled my eyes and looked in my phone. I was done with love for a minute, so hearing him spit his lying ass game was irritating.

"True wants you." The girl he went upstairs with rolled her eyes and looked at me with her arms folded.

I took a deep breath and got up.

"Where he at?" I asked.

"Up the stairs." She looked me up and down and then stepped off.

"Fuck wrong with that hoe?" I walked off and went up the stairs to a steel door.

It opened as soon as I stepped up to it. It was a bedroom, neat and clean for a nigga too.

"Sit down," True said after closing the door.

"What you want, nigga?" I asked, feeling weird about sitting on his bed.

"I want you to sit down. Didn't you hear me?" he scrunched his eyebrows.

Oh, this nigga's mouth.

"I know you used to dealin' with these bucket heads that let you run them with that attitude, but I ain't the one, honey." I cocked my head to the side.

"Yeah, you is. Sit down." He pulled a chair in front of me as I flopped on the bed.

"The fuck you doin' out here?" he asked.

"You know what I'm doin' out here."

"Nah, I don't." He lit up a fat blunt.

"So, that's why you bein' all rude?" I asked.

"You don't even know, do you?" He handed me the blunt, and I took it.

"I know what the fuck I can do. You only sayin' that shit cuz I'm a female." I flared my nostrils.

"Nah, it's not that. Your cousin is proof of that shit. But you, I think you could do other shit. I already spoke to your pops about it, and he agreed," he said.

I bucked my eyes.

"Nigga, don't be goin' behind—" I started to scream, but

he grabbed my cheeks and pulled my face to an inch away from his.

"I don't like loud ass females. You too pretty to be runnin' ya mouth like that. Now let me finish talkin', and then you can talk." He looked down at my lips like he wanted to kiss me.

I wanted to lean in, but this nigga had me fucked up.

"Let me go," I said, feeling like I looked dumb because my lips were pushed together.

He let me go, and I tried to slap him, and but he grabbed my arms and pushed me back on the bed.

"You fuckin' crazy?" he asked.

"No, but you must fuckin' be." I tried to kick, but he had me locked down.

"If you was my bitch, I swear. I would fix that mouth for your ass," he said in my ear.

I felt like I couldn't even breathe and it wasn't from all the pressure his weight put on me. It was his presence. It was strong.

"Well, I ain't, so get off me." My breathing had gotten faint.

True's body felt so good on mine. He put his face in my neck and started planting small kisses on it. I felt paralyzed and my nipples became erect because of the waves he was sending.

"True, I left my phone." The chick he was with walked in.

"You ain't see the door closed?" he asked her.

"Really? You brought me to your house, nigga, and ain't give me no dick, but you in here ready to fuck on this hoe?" She looked devastated.

"Um, ain't nobody fuckin', and nigga, get off me." I looked at him and he had a cute ass smirk on his face.

"Shorty, you need to close the door. I'm talkin'," he said then picked her phone up and handed it to her.

He stroked her face and kissed her.

"I'ma be back down," he said.

Oh my God, this nigga was smooth as fuck. Shit, my stupid ass pussy got wet for him.

"Y'all can have the room." I got up and tried to pass him, but he grabbed me around me waist.

Lord have mercy, when he touch me he run me. I needed to leave. This was Chino cousin.

The chick walked out, and he closed the door back.

"Look, your father agreed we should put you on some small shit, you know. So, we think you can handle the weed, molly, shit like that. I got you a lil army already, so you need to let them niggas know you the bitch to see or they won't respect you. I see you already got a lil crew tho," he said.

"Yeah, my cousin and her team legit." I pursed my lips.

"You need anything, let me know." He let my waist go, but shit, I didn't even want him to.

"This your spot?" I asked, walking past him.

"Yeah. Like a lil club house, you know. So, what's your plan out here? Tryna find a dude or sum?" he asked.

"No, I ain't tryna fuck wit no nigga after your cuz. I might have to be gay now." I laughed.

"All niggas ain't bad." He smirked and showed the dimples in his cheeks.

"Well, I wouldn't know."

I went down the stairs and saw Pashia was gone and so was Lucci.

"What the hell," I said, stopping where we sat.

I looked around for Dela, and she was now in the corner sitting on the dude's lap that she met outside. I walked to the back and hoped Pashia was in the bathroom somewhere because her ass drove. I went to a door and opened it, only to find Fatima face deep, eating that stripper's pussy from the back.

I slammed the door and stepped off. I called Pashia's phone, and it went to voicemail.

"Oh, nah," I scoffed.

I walked over to Dela, and she handed me a blunt. I pulled it and held it in.

"Where the hell Pashia go?" I asked.

"Oh, she told me to give you her keys and you could take the car. I'ma roll with big sexy." She rubbed on the guy.

"Aight, cool," I said and handed her the weed back.

I decided to go finish off one of those bottles they had at the table. True was sitting there alone looking through his phone. I grabbed the bottle, and the sound of the ice shifting made him look up. I damn near shuddered because still felt those kisses on my neck.

"You made yourself comfy at the king's table, I see." He handed me a clean glass.

"I mean, I'ma be the queen soon... Bloop." I laughed.

"My queen?" He picked up his cup and looked at me.

"Boy," I said, but my ass was like *yes, daddy* inside.

"I just fuckin' wit you. Pour up. Matter of fact, drink this shit." He pulled up a bottle of Dom.

"Nigga tryna hide the good shit." I giggled and held my glass out as he poured.

"There your ass go." The chick Vee came stomping up to True. She looked at me with her eyebrows raised.

"Ohh nigga, so I knew I was right. You was feelin' this bitch that night," she said and pointed at me.

"Shorty, you wildin' right now. I can have who I want in my shit. Calm down." He stood up.

I sipped my drink and watched.

"I ain't doin' shit," she screamed in his face.

He snatched her arm "Bitch, I said calm down," he barked.

"Nigga, fuck you. I swear, I'm so sick of these hoes and you, True," she carried on.

"I'll bust your ass over the head with this bottle and toss your ass out. Now, I said, shut the fuck up," he said, and that nigga voice was a boom.

"Fuck you lookin' at, hoe?" Vee said, looking at me.

"A bitch that's about to walk her goofy ass up them steps." I laughed.

Vee turned up her lip and stomped up the stairs.

True looked at me.

"You gon' be here when I get back?" He smiled.

"Hell no, I'm boutta roll after I finish this drink." I went in my phone.

"Shit, the way you drinkin', your ass is gon' be here." He laughed and went up the stairs.

I shook my head and continued to drink his shit up. The party started to die down, and I was drunk as fuck. I tried to get up but couldn't even move.

"Shit."

I lay back, and my ass drifted off to sleep.

I woke up and couldn't even remember how the hell I got home. Then I looked around and saw I wasn't home. I heard snoring, and I screamed when I saw a nigga lying next to me with his back turned. *Oh my God, did I get drunk and a nigga took advantage?* It was still dark, but I could start to make out the room. It was True's spot. I leaned over and saw it was him sleeping.

"True." I shook him, and he turned over.

"What, man?" he said groggily.

"Did we fuck?" I asked.

"Fuck no, you was sleep, and I put your ass in the bed. I wasn't about to sleep on the couch in my own shit." He turned over and pulled his covers over him.

I was still fully dressed.

"Thanks. I'm sorry." I got up, and he grabbed my arm.

"It's cool. You feel like makin' me some breakfast?" he asked.

This nigga was bold as fuck. He ain't know my ass for shit and talking about make him some breakfast. Like, first of all, nigga, what's in the fridge?

"Damn, okay." I laughed.

"I mean, we can go get somethin' if you don't feel like it." He got up and stretched.

"I can make somethin' real fast." I got up.

I didn't know why I felt comfortable now or something. I guess we felt each other last night. He was cool, and them neck kisses ain't hurt, I gave him that. he was still rude in my eyes, though.

"I got a fresh tank top and some sweats that are too small for me in the closet if you wanna get out that dress, ma." He got up, and he ain't have on shit but his boxers.

I tried not to look at his dick print, but man. His body was beautiful and covered in tats, his arms, chest, stomach and back.

"Shorty, you my cousin's bitch. Stop lookin' so hard." He laughed.

"I ain't his bitch. I wish you stop sayin' that," I said.

"So, I can fuck you?" he asked, grabbing his dick.

That shit made my pussy throb.

"Um no, the fact that I'm his ex is a law." I laughed.

"Exactly, see what I mean?" He chuckled himself.

"Whatever."

I went and got the sweats I assumed he was talking about and grabbed a tank top out the drawer. He came in behind me and grabbed a towel and some underwear. I tried to move quickly, but I still felt his body against mine.

I ran the hell out that closet and went downstairs. The place was spotless. All those niggas were in there last night, so how the fuck he get this shit clean?

I went to the kitchen and opened the fridge. This nigga's shit was stocked like he had stamps. I grabbed some Eckrich beef sausage, eggs, cheese, and butter. I saw he had a flip waffle iron, so I went in the pantry and saw there was pancake/waffle mix and whipped the shit up. After I was done, I plated the food and set some orange juice on the table.

True came downstairs looking like a fucking meal in his jogger sweats, and he was shirtless. His studs glistened on his ears, and his *I'm tired* face was sexy. Lord help a bitch out right now.

"This shit looks good." He sat down and grabbed the syrup. "Thank you." He looked at me and I nodded.

"It's hard to find young joints that still cook," he said and bit into the waffles. "You threw some strawberries in these bitches?" He smiled.

That was my favorite, strawberry waffles.

"Yeah." I giggled at how he was enjoying the food.

"So, what's your story?" he asked.

"I wanted to be dumb, so I was dumb." I shrugged.

"We all dumb sometimes, ma. Lil shorty, Vee, is wild but I can't stop fuckin' with her ass."

That shit raised some envy.

"She your girl?" I asked.

"Not really, she married." He looked at his phone and set it down.

"So why you don't just get your own shorty?" I asked as I poured syrup on my waffles.

"Ion know. I ain't got that one chick yet." He started in on the eggs.

"Oh." I picked up the remote and turned on the TV that sat on the counter.

"About that shit last night, I got a list of mufuckas you gon' be sending shit out to. You need to get to know them well, aight? They loyal," he said, talking business again.

I just watched him talk and eat. Why couldn't I have met him instead of Chino's ass?

After we ate, we smoked and shit, then I knew it was time to leave. He put on a movie, and I had a feeling that sitting next to him too long would make me a hoe.

"Shit, we gon' be eating lunch soon," he said while we watched *Pineapple Express.*

"It's cool. I took too much of your time already." I got up and grabbed Pashia's keys.

"I ain't have shit to do today, if you wanted to chill longer," True said, walking me to the door.

I had a feeling he was enjoying my company as much as I was his.

"Honestly, I would, but for some reason I feel like we can't do this type of shit." I nervously giggled.

"Shit, we gon' be working together. We can be cool. Unless you want me too bad, and that's when I gotta, you know..." He made a curve motion.

"Oh, nigga, you too cocky." I laughed.

"Nah, but for real. You cool, I see why Chino fell for you. You a good shorty."

"See what I mean? Don't compliment me and stuff." I was sure I was blushing now.

"Girl, go on. I'll see you around." He walked away when he heard his phone ringing.

I watched him for a minute before I closed the door and leaned on the other side. When I finally walked off to get into Pashia's car, I was all smiles. He made me feel plain old good inside.

I pulled off, and just as I did, I saw Chino speeding past me.

"Oh shit."

I started to get pissed. Was this nigga True tryna set me the fuck up?

TRUE

I watched Passion's fine ass get in the car and pull off. I knew I shouldn't have asked her to stay and all that shit, but man, when I saw her last night, I knew she was meant to be around a nigga. I wasn't no snake ass nigga, but she had that vibe I liked about a female, only better. She was dope, and I knew it. I replied to the text from Vee that she sent when me and Passion was cooling.

Knock, Knock

I pulled out my piece when I heard a knock on the door. I wasn't expecting anyone, so nobody should be there.

"Who is it?" I called out.

"Your cousin, nigga," he said through the door.

"Chino, the fuck." I opened the door, and he stood there smoking a blunt.

"What's good, cuzo? Let a nigga in," he said and walked in.

"What you doin' up here?" I asked.

"I heard my shorty was out here and decided to come talk to her. I stopped here first to let you know I was in town and to get the hoes ready." He laughed.

"Nigga, I had a party last night. Paid them hoes a stack to clean the shit up so I ain't have to see it in the morning." I went in the fridge and grabbed a water.

"I was thinkin' about movin' up here, cuz. You know, get on with the New Freezer boys," he said.

"That's cool, but you gotta earn your way into the New Freezer boys, cuz. It ain't about blood," I told him. Damn, a minute later, and he would had seen Passion. "Aye, gimme a minute," I said, walking into the bathroom after seeing Passion's name come up on my text. I had saved it the other day.

I opened it while walking into the bathroom.

Passion: So you planned on him coming to catch me there?

I turned my lip up.

Me: I don't play fuck games sweetheart. I ain't know the nigga was comin'.

Passion: Yeah, okay. You cool, and I wanna keep us cool.

I laughed because she tried to talk to me tough, but I ain't bite.

Me: lmaooo bye shorty

I went back into the living room.

"I gotta run, cuz. You wanna go with me? I just got her address."

"From who?" I wondered.

"Oh, my homie, Marco. He works for the light company," he said.

"Well, nah, I'm home, nigga, so I can't go playin' and shit. Holla at me later," I told him.

I needed to get to my actual home. I had to meet up with my mother and my sister.

"Cool. I'm glad I caught your ass here and ain't have to search. You ain't never tell me where your new spot at," he said

"Yeah, cuz, I don't want you robbin' me, nigga." I laughed.

"I got paper, nigga. I don't need yours." He deuced me and left.

I laughed and went upstairs to grab my keys and shit. Passion had left her clothes and walked out with my sweats and shit, so I grabbed them up and put them in a bag for her.

There was another knock on the door when I was about to leave.

"Man, what the fuck goin' on today?" I said to myself as I walked to the door and looked out.

I rolled my eyes.

"Vee, I ain't with that bullshit today." I opened the door and walked into the living room space.

"I'm pregnant," she blurted out.

I scrunched my face up and turned to her.

"The fuck you mean? I strap up. That's your husband's

baby, ma." I walked to the counter and grabbed my sheets and funnel.

"I haven't had sex with him in months because he's always gone on them business trips. It's yours. I ain't fuckin' nobody else," she said.

"Well, what the fuck you gonna do, shorty?" I walked out the door as she followed.

"I wanna have your baby, True. I'm gonna keep it," she said.

This shit was suspect as fuck because I always strapped up, and the two times we didn't, I made her ass eat a Plan B.

"So, you gon be married to another nigga and try to raise my baby behind his back? It sounds crazy." I leaned back on my car and rolled my shit up.

"I was thinking maybe I could tell him it's his, but you know it's yours, so it shouldn't matter."

I snatched her to me and stared into her soul.

"I ain't never take you for a dumb bitch for real, but that's the dumbest shit I think you ever said to me. It's fucked up you even think I would roll with that foul shit. Bitch, get an abortion or tell the nigga. Oh, and I want a test." I let her go and got in the car.

She looked hurt, but I honestly didn't give a fuck because she knew better than to come at me like I'm some clown ass fuck nigga who makes kids and don't love them. Fuck out outta here.

I made it to Tribeca and pulled in front of my house. My

mother's car was already there. I got out, jogged up the stairs, and opened the first set of doors, then the next.

"Ma." I walked in the kitchen when I smelled cake.

"You know I was gon' cook for my baby." She smiled.

My mother was Gabbie Luvher. Chino's mother and my mother were sisters. They hated each other too. They were identical twins, but they were opposite as hell. My mother was sweet and deadly, while Chino's mother, Abbie, was an evil, psycho bitch at times. Her and her drunk ass nigga.

"I already know. Where Queen at?" I asked. Queen was my sister. She was a year younger than me.

"She upstairs going through your stuff, probably. You know her boyfriend blacked her eyes again. Imma kill that lil muthafucka." She seethed.

"Man, we told her to chill on ole boy, and she won't. That's her problem now." I shrugged.

I tried to help my sister, but she was wild and dumb as fuck.

"Bro bro." Queen walked in wearing a pair of shorts all the way up in her pussy and a sports bra.

"The fuck," I said to her

"Nigga please, I'm on the way to the gym." She placed her hand on her hip.

"Yeah, okay. Anyway, what you wanted to talk to us about, Ma?" I asked her.

"I need y'all to help me with this party for your father," she said.

"That nigga ain't my father. That's her father," I said.

"He been in your life since your ass was a year old," my mother said.

"Well, he always treated me different, so I act different."

After my pops got killed, that nigga got my mother pregnant quick. He was his best friend. My uncle told me the whole story when I turned fifteen.

"What you need?" I said, trying to rush the shit.

"What I need is for you to show some damn respect, True. Ghani took care of you like his own. He a good dude, and you know that shit," she said and pointed at me.

"Aight, Ma," I said, not trying to sit and hear this shit all day. I loved my mother but she would go round for round over that nigga.

"I wanna do one of those seventies parties." She smiled brightly. "Let's find a big hall, and we can get it decorated in a seventies theme. So, we gotta keep it secret. Queen, take care of the DJ and find the hall. And son, I need you to get a caterer, cake, and the bartender," she said as she frosted the strawberry cake.

"And what you gon' do?" I smirked.

"I got my own thing to do, don't you worry," she said.

"I'ma need half that," I said and pointed at the cake.

She made all her cakes from scratch. Shit, she was why I needed a female who can cook and who keep that pussy clean. I was a big nigga, and I needed to eat, whether food or pussy.

We sat and talked a lil bit. I did what I said and ate half

that cake. Shit was hittin' too. After they left, I felt my phone vibrate and saw I had to get to the spot they sent my.

My phone vibrated again, and I saw it was Passion, which had me curious.

Passion: My bad about earlier. I ain't mean to accuse you.

Me: You good, shorty.

Passion: Okay cool. That party was crazy.

It was like she was trying to keep a conversation going. *I can't like this girl.*

Me: Yeah, we gon do some more shit like that if y'all wanna stomp thru.

Passion: Okay let me know when

I didn't message back because a nigga like me would have been like, *aye shorty, slide through,* and I ain't wanna do that shit, but I did. I ended up calling Medina to see what she was up to.

"Wassup, I ain't heard from you since we got back," she said when she picked up.

"Yeah, I know, but what you up to?" I asked.

Medina was my cousin and homie. We always got fucked up together and shit. I wasn't on shit right now, so that would be cool.

"Ain't shit, up here chillin' with Chino. He up here sick about Passion." She laughed.

"Oh aight, I'm boutta come through." I hung up.

I looked at Passion's text and almost hit her ass up. Nah, I was cool.

AFTER CHECKING myself out in the mirror, I grabbed the black card out the safe in my closet and quickly left the house. It was time to reup, and I needed to get my shipment and send it out. This shit was dope. I realized I had been doing it all wrong for years. This system is off the hook.

I made it to Queens and parked down the block. When I got to the address, which was an office building that had a nail shop and hair salon at the store front, I knew they wouldn't send me through the business, so I went to the side and saw a grey door. They moved spots every time from what I had seen so far.

I slid my key, and the door opened. I walked through two security check points before I got into the "Store." It was literally a drug store, any drug you need. All I had to do was check my orders, pick up the barcode for what I needed, and they basically checked me out, which was me scanning my card to show what I picked up. It even calculated how much money I should get after flipping it.

"We gon' drop tonight to everybody, and you'll get the confirmations," the girl who checked me out said.

"Cool." I nodded.

After I checked out, I sent a mass text that simply said, *Freezer*. That let all my clients know we was good and to be ready.

I was leaving out when I smelled that perfume. Passion was there. I saw her by the pills and figured she took heed to what I told her. I ain't sayin' shorty couldn't have a come up, but she needed to start from the bottom and work her way up. I didn't bother to say shit to her, but I caught her eye just as I was leaving.

I couldn't shake my attraction to her for shit, but I knew I had to make sure I tried to keep shit friendly and business. She was one of them bitches you just had to touch. I got in my whip and rolled up. I knew me. Shit, I was a nigga at the end of the day, and that bitch made my dick hard.

"Hey," I heard Passion call out before I pulled off.

"What's good, ma?" I asked rolling my window down.

"I know your ass saw me, nigga." She laughed.

"I did."

"Dang, nigga, you act like we wasn't chillin' yesterday. You don't fuck with me now?" She cocked her head to the side.

I couldn't help but smile a little.

"Nah, it's not that, ma." I chuckled.

"Well look, I got dropped off my Pashia since I still had her car. Can you give me a ride?" she asked.

"Aight." I got out, and she backed up.

"Fuck you scared for?" I said, looking down at her.

She looked away and walked to open the passenger door, but I quickly opened it for her.

"Thanks, I ain't know you was gentleman." She beamed.

"I'm not." I smirked and closed the door once she slid in.

"So, where you stay?" I asked, pulling off.

"I don't even know how to get there from here. Let me put my address in."

"Learn the streets," I told her.

"I am, I'ma get it. Shit, I ain't been here but a lil bit."

Her phone started ringing, and she looked immediately pissed.

"Chino, leave me the fuck alone," she said, trying to turn to her right like I couldn't hear her. "Well, why the hell you here? You better not be at my place, Chino," she said and hung up.

"You good?" I asked, knowing she wasn't.

"No."

"You wanna go home?" I asked her.

"Not really, but he wouldn't know where I live anyway."

"I was about to stop at a lil' chicken spot and grab something. That breakfast wore off," I said.

"Damn, some chicken does sound good." She bounced her arms.

I loved how playful shorty was too.

"Aight, I got you, ma."

She smiled, and I got this feeling in my chest. I ain't like that shit.

"Let's grab it to go," I said, ready to get away from her ass. She did something to me.

"Aight, let's take it to your club house." She giggled.

"Fuck," I said and pulled over.

I had to do this shit.

"What's wro—" Passion started, but I grabbed the back

of her head and pulled her face to mine. My tongue went deep into her mouth. We kissed long and hard, and I began to get horny as fuck.

"Shit." She pulled back.

"What's wrong?" I said and leaned back in, but she stopped me.

"We can't do this. I'm your cousin—"

"What? You his what?" I asked, calling her ass out.

"True..." she said, and I sped off.

I should have gone with my gut and just not did shit. I didn't even say shit the rest of the drive. We went to the chicken spot and grabbed the food, but we ate it there.

"I'm sorry if I made you feel some type of way." She stared at me across the table as I looked in my phone.

"True," she said when I didn't answer her.

"Shorty, I'm good, aight? I shouldn't have done it," I said, still not looking at her.

"You can look at me, you know," she said, sounding like she was getting mad.

I just smirked.

She got up and stomped out the door. I laughed and got up behind her.

"Shorty, what you so hot about?" I asked as I followed her down the street.

"I ain't." She turned around with her arms folded.

"Then why you leave?"

"Because you don't have to be mad at me, True. We just met for real, and...." She stopped.

"And what?" I asked, stepping closer in her space.

"I don't know why I like you, but it's wrong. When I met you, it was instant, and I can't do shit about it," she said, looking at me and biting her lip.

"Come here." I unfolded her arms and used her shirt to pull her to my chest. "I like your ass too." I kissed her, and this time she didn't pull back.

My phone rang, causing us to break the kiss.

"Yeah." I picked up for Lucci but didn't take my eyes off Passion.

"Where you at, bro?" he said with a lot of noise in the background.

"I'm out chillin'. What's good?" I asked.

"Aye, nigga, we out here. Come fuck with ya boys, B. We in Marcy, and we got the court lit."

"Aight, I'ma be there," I said and hung up.

"You ready to drop me off?" Passion asked.

"Nah, not really. You ready to break out?"

"No."

"Well, come chill with me and my folks," I offered.

"Aight, lemme hit my cousin and see if she gon' be there," she said and took out her phone.

"You don't trust me? You ain't gotta have back up around me." I chuckled.

"Whatever." She smiled.

We drove over, and Lucci was wild as hell. This crazy nigga had a whole block party going on. He had grills burning, Icee stands, and shit.

"Damn, y'all always do it like this?" Passion asked.

"Hell yeah, New Freezer Boys, shorty." I wrapped my arm around her waist, and she blushed.

"Aye, True." Lucci stepped to us as we got closer.

"What's up, bruh." We slapped hands.

"How you doin' Ms. Lady. Y'all came together?" Lucci's hot ass asked.

"Duh, nigga. Shorty came to get the vibe."

"Oh, aight, cool. Let's do the mufucka." Lucci held up his bottle.

I sat on the top of the bench, and Passion sat down between my legs. I know that shit probably seemed fucked up, but I was feeling her ass, and now I knew she was feeling a nigga. I ain't know what this shit was between us, but it felt good as fuck.

1 week later

"Thank y'all so much. This shit is nice."

My mother looked around the ballroom I got for us in a country club out in Tribeca. I made it all happen and got the food catered from this Italian spot. I looked at Queen, who was on her phone looking like she was about to cry. I heard her arguing with that fuck boy earlier and decided to not let that shit be my business.

"Okay, in ten minutes he gon' be here, okay?" Ma said.

"Aight, cool. I'ma get them to hit the disco lights," I told her.

The shit was a flashback in time. Not that I would know. Shit, I was only 25.

"Queen, you need to come on and help me get the gifts neat." My mother walked over to the side where Queen was.

I called Yanai, my date for the night. She was my good girl. I only fucked with her when I felt like it, and she was cool with the shit. She was in college, and since I paid for it, I wanted her to focus.

"Hey, True, I'm almost there," she said with her sexy ass voice.

I loved hearing her talk. She had that light voice. My line beeped, and I saw it was Chino calling. He said he would swing by.

"What's good, kid?" I said, hanging up on Yanai.

"I'm on the way up there. It's cool for shorty to come?" he asked.

"Who?" I questioned.

"Who you think? Passion, nigga," he said.

I scoffed thinking about how she talked all that hard shit about being done with him.

"That's cool," I said and hung up.

"He coming," I heard my mother's thick, raspy voice call out.

The lights went dim, and as soon as Ghani opened the door, every screamed, "Surprise!"

His Danny Glover looking ass held his chest in surprise.

"Oh, man." He grabbed my mother and kissed her then hugged Queen.

"Y'all crazy," he said and shook my hand.

"It's cool, old man." I gave a smirk.

Ghani's side of the family ran up to him. His cousins and his grandkids were there. He had three kids of his own before he got with my mother. All three of his sons were there too

"There you are." Yanai came up and leapt into my arms.

"Hey, shorty." I wrapped my arms around her and kissed her neck.

"Hey, sweetheart. Haven't seen you in a while."

My mother walked up and hugged Yanai. She always liked her because she wasn't no hood rat type, and she had goals.

"Thanks, Ms. Gabbie." Yanai smiled.

I admired her bell bottoms and halter. She had on a bush and some big ass hoops. She looked cute as fuck.

"I'ma have to get you out this bitch," I said in her ear.

Her face turned red as she blushed.

"Cuzzin," I heard Chino say. "Hey, Auntie." He hugged my mother.

I saw Passion and my damn heart almost stopped. She had on this spandex two piece skirt set with her hair in a long, braided ponytail. Fuck. We hadn't talked at all or seen each other since that that night we kissed and shit. I started to feel like she was avoiding me and shit, but I ain't press it.

"Hey." She smiled, and I gritted on her ass.

Shit pissed me off. She didn't know she was better than how she was treated.

"Let's go get some drinks, bae."

I pulled on Yanai, and we walked off. I ain't mean to carry her like that, but she pissed me off. I tried not to be around them, but Chino couldn't stay away from me. I could tell how I behaved threw Passion off. I got up and went to the bathroom, leaving everybody at the table to eat.

I was actually going in there to smoke. I locked the door, and as soon as I lit up, someone knocked.

"I'm in here. The fuck," I said.

"I know, nigga. That's why I'm knocking," I heard Passion say.

I opened the door, and she rushed in.

"So, what the fuck? I thought we was cool. You tryna flex on me cuz you got some bitch witchu? Oh nah," she said and snatched my weed.

I was stunned and ain't even know how to react to her ass.

"Ain't nobody flexin' on you. I see you back with Chino." I sat on the small waiting chair.

"First of all, I ain't back with him. He asked me to come, and to be honest, I was actually hoping to see your ass. But now I wish the fuck I would have stayed home." She handed me the weed and opened the door to leave.

"The fuck you need to see me about?" I said, pushing the door back closed and locking it.

"I don't know. I thought we was kind of feeling each other on some friend shit... I mean. Ughhh." She grunted. "I was just hoping to feel like that again, like on some friend shit." She shrugged.

"Aaaw, shorty wanna be my friend and shit." I laughed.

"Oh my God, shut up." She laughed, and that shit made my dick hard.

"My bad, aight. I can be an asshole, I hear."

"Mhhhmm," she said, holding her hand out for me to shake.

"You funny."

I pulled her in for a hug, and for some reason, I couldn't let go. Then I noticed she hadn't either. I looked down at her then slowly leaned in and pressed my lips to hers. I pulled her bottom lip into my mouth and slipped my tongue in the space. I ain't wanna stop, so I didn't.

"Shit," she said and started falling down.

"What the fuck?" I said, going down to help her.

I tried to help her up, but she just kept falling; shorty got weak.

"We can't do that," she said, catching her balance.

"Do what?" I gripped her neck and roughly kissed her as I grabbed on every fluffy part that was squeezable.

"True...." She moaned as I kissed down the side of her face to her neck.

Knock, Knock, Knock

"Fuck," I said and pecked Passion's lips.

"We can't do this," she repeated. "I feel the same shit you do, but its foul," she said.

The person at the door stopped knocking.

"Then why you ain't stop me?" I asked and walked out.

Chino was sitting in the corner while some bitch was all in his ear and shit. I shook my head and walked back over to join my family.

I was fucked up the rest of the night. I took Yanai home and tried to split her ass in two while thinking about Passion's ass. I wanted her, and I couldn't fight the shit, so I wasn't going to.

PASSION

I was overheated the whole drive home. I looked over at Chino and punched him in the face.

"Bitch, what the fuck you do that for?" he screamed.

"Because I fuckin' hate you. I don't even know why I came. Why you here, Chino? To lie and shit in my face?" I screamed.

"Why the fuck you ain't do all this when I came to your spot? The fuck you wait until now for, shorty? You could have argued wit' me earlier," he said while holding his face.

I was taking my feeling for True out on him.

My phone started ringing, and I immediately answered when I saw Pashia's name.

"Hey, cuz," I answered.

"Bitch, you need to get down to that new spot we opened. Those lil niggas robbed the shit and killed one of my bitches," she said out of breath and angry.

"What? Oh, bitch, I'm on the way," I said.

"The fuck wrong?" Chino asked.

"Some shit happened that I gotta handle," I said.

"What you mean?" he asked.

He didn't know the reason I was there.

"I'm one of the newest New York plugs, nigga. I ain't just your bitch, I always knew I was more," I said to him.

He burst out laughing, and my face remained solid.

"The fuck you know about moving weight?" He laughed again.

"Keep laughing. Ask your cousin who the fuck I am, nigga," I said getting an attitude.

"You serious?" he said.

"Yeah, dead serious. I need your car."

"I'll take you," he said.

"Aight, whatever," I said and gave him directions.

Once I stepped out, my workers ran up and all tried at once to tell me what happened.

"Oh shit you was dead serious," Chino said as he watched the commotion.

"Passion, I heard it was one of them niggas from uptown. I saw the tattoo on one of they hand," Dela said.

"And, bitch, we about to go hard. We need to get the shit back," Pashia said, stepping closer. She looked at Chino "Ain't this—" she started.

"Yeah," I said. "Look, y'all go handle that shit. Get my fuckin weight back, and when y'all find the nigga who made the play, save him for me," I told them. "I ain't playin' fuck games, and niggas think cuz we bitches, we can't handle our own." I stopped to look at Chino. "But we can, and we about to show these mufuckas who the..."

I stopped and looked at my all female crew.

"The Dirty Diamond Girls. They gon' know who the fuck the Dirty Diamond Girls are. Get the shit done and make sure a message is sent," I told them.

"I like that shit, cuz. The Dirty Diamond Girls!" Pashia raised her hands, and everybody cheered.

"Let's go," I told them, and they all scattered, jumping in different cars.

"Damn, ma," Chino said as we got back in the car.

"What?" I said, leaning back in my seat.

"I ain't never seen you like this," he said.

"Good, that means I'm doin' better without you," I said, snapping back to my attitude.

He inhaled deeply and drove back to my building.

"Can I come use the bathroom?" he asked.

"Chino, you just tryna get back in my place. Just go back to Philly."

"I'm moving up here," he said.

"Why the fuck you following me, Chino?"

I got out, and I heard his car door close behind me. I tried to get on the elevator fast, but he caught it and got on. I rolled my eyes as the elevator rose.

"So, you tryna say we really over?" Chino asked.

"Yes, we're really over. How you think that shit gon' fly?" I asked him. "You treated me like shit for years, and my dumb ass stayed. Not this time. I'm done, and moving on," I yelled.

He hit the stop button on the elevator.

"Moving on with who?" he asked.

"Just moving on period." I leaned on the wall.

"Baby, come here." He kissed me, but I pushed him off.

"Don't touch me, Chino. I only went with you to this thing because I thought my cousin would show up," I lied.

He ignored me and started kissing me again. I went around him and pulled the stop button.

"Don't do it again, or we gon' fight," I told him.

Once I got to my floor, I got off and rushed to my door.

"Passion, you know I can't be without you for long," he said and walked up behind me.

I scoffed and turned to face him.

"See what I mean? The fact that you can be without me at all is the reason I know you don't want me, you just want to have me."

I quickly opened my door and slammed it. It locked automatically when my key pod passed through the threshold.

"Passion." He banged on the door, and I walked away and went to my room.

I didn't have time for his head games. He had committed the most atrocious crimes of the heart, and with my best friend, too. It made me pissed all over again. I stripped down and ran a bubble bath.

I turned on my music and grabbed the sound bar

remote for the bathroom. I played Cardi B's *Invasion of Privacy* and laid back looking through my phone. I went on Snap and took a picture with the bubbles around me. Then, I shared it to IG. Within a few minutes, I got a text.

True: *Take that shit down.*

He sent a screen shot of my picture.

I started laughing.

Me: *Nigga, first of all, how the fuck you on my IG? And second, I'm grown.*

True: *Send shit like that to me, not to the world.*

My heart started pounding, and I felt like I couldn't breathe.

My phone began to ring, and it was True.

"Oh fuck, fuck, fuck," I said, about to pass out.

"Hello." I tried to answer like I wasn't hyperventilating.

"You was takin' too long."

"You funny, so what's up?" I said.

"You tell me. I mean, where my pic at, though?" He coughed like he was smoking.

"I ain't gonna send my pics to you so you can show all your friends and shit," I said with a fake attitude.

"I'm a grown ass man, girl. I want that shit to be all me, so why would I do that?" he said. "I'm boutta come over. I got some gas too, so lets chill," he said like he was moving around.

"How you just gon' invite your ass over here?" I said.

"Girl, you got a code or some shit for the building?"

I heard his car chime like he opened the door.

"Your ass is crazy," I said.

"I guess I gotta figure it out myself." He hung up.

I started laughing because his ass was tripping.

Shaking my head, I hit next on the music and continued my bath. As I grabbed the towel off the rack, I must have been hungry because I could have sworn I smelled seafood or something. I was gonna order me some damn food.

After throwing on my robe I walked out and headed into my bedroom. I backed up when something down the hall caught my eye. It was a pair of shoes under my dining room table. I walked in and saw at the other end of the table was True watching TV while eating shrimp and shit.

"Um, nigga..." I placed my hands on my hips.

"You took forever. Your crab legs gon' be cold as shit," he said with seafood spread all over the table. Crab legs, fried shrimp, lobster tails, and shit.

"How the hell you get in?" I asked.

"I'm True. You don't know me yet, so it's cool," he said and pulled the chair out for me to sit down.

"I'm surprised you got pulled away from your lil date." I smirked.

"Oh, you jealous?" He smiled. "I just dropped her off. She was mad as shit when I called you," he said.

"You so fuckin' rude." I shook my head and dug in that food.

"Nah, she already knows what's up with me."

"And what's up with you?" I retorted.

"Nothin'. I don't play with my money, I don't play wit

these niggas, and I don't play with these bitches. She knows if she was my bitch, I would have never done it. But she just my piece, feel me? I got respect for her and shit, tho," he said and slid over some butter.

"Well, how respectful is that?" I laughed.

"Boutta the closest she gon' get," he said seriously.

"You never had that one broad you wanted to be with forever?" I asked.

"Yeah," he simply said.

"And?" I used my hand to motion for him to continue.

"She died." He looked at the TV.

"I'm sorry," I said, wishing I didn't press him.

"It's cool, ma. I miss her like shit, though," he said.

"Wow. Damn, now I don't even know what to say,"

"You can tell me why you ain't eating that high ass food in front of you." He laughed.

"Ooop," I said and picked up the crab legs.

"You remind me of her," he said, breaking the short silence.

"Really?" I asked.

"Yeah, your whole demeanor. That ride or die shit, you the truth," he said, wiping his hands and getting up.

"I need to wash my hands," he said.

"Down the hall," I said as our eyes locked.

I looked back down and tried to eat but couldn't. True walked back in and handed me my phone.

"It was ringing," he said and sat down.

"Thanks, but your ass could have used the hallway bathroom," I said, realizing he must have gone into my bedroom.

"Nah, I wanted to see where I was gon' be sleepin' and shit." He sat down and started drinking down his Gatorade.

"Wait, what?" I cocked my head.

"You heard me. You slept in mine, so my turn, ma." He tapped my knee, but once he touched it, he didn't let it go.

"You just got out the tub." He bit down on his bottom lip.

"Yeah," I said with a shivering voice as his hand reached higher up my thigh.

I was still ass naked with my robe on. Once his fingers reached my pussy, I was done. He slid his fingers in and out of me.

"True, fuuuck." I moaned.

"What?" he said, moving closer and opening my robe, exposing my titties.

"Maaaan." He licked his lips and went straight for my nipples.

My pussy was soaked.

True started circling my clit, and it seemed to push me over. I came on his fingers. He didn't even give me a chance to recover before he picked me up and carried me into the bedroom.

"Ain't no take backs." He laid me down and pulled my robe off.

I didn't give a fuck. Chino could kiss my ass.

"I won't," I said as I pulled at his belt and snatched his jeans down and his underwear.

His dick sprang up and hit me in the chin. We both started laughing. He pulled out a Magnum and slid it over that big motherfucker with too much effort. I thought the bitch might pop. He needed XL.

True leaned in and kissed me slowly. His tongue felt so good against mine. I could feel the head of his dick, and I closed my eyes once he filled me up. My back arched, and I almost screamed.

"Take it, girl," True sexily grunted in my ear and covered my lips with his.

He pushed both my legs back and slammed into me hard and deep. I felt like I was throwing up gang signs with my fingers.

"Damn... Tr-tr-t-t-t," I stuttered.

"Shit, I sent you retarded." He chuckled but continued the dick slaying.

He pulled out and flipped me over, but he basically put me in a split and then busted my pussy open. He had my waist in a death grip, and he tore my shit down. I was lost as fuck in minutes and cumming like a crazy bitch. This nigga could easily get a bitch hooked.

"Ride it." He slapped my ass cheeks hard.

"Okay," I said, completely worn out.

"The fuck you just say?" He grabbed me gently by the neck.

"I said okay." I was still breathing heavily.

"Nah, say 'Yes, True.'" He slid me down on his dick before I could talk shit.

"Now, ride it." He squeezed my thigh.

"Yes, True!" He started fucking me back, and I was cumming again.

"Fuck, your shit tight," he said as he banged my walls.

"Shit, I'm boutta cum, ma." He quickly got up and held me up.

I wrapped my legs around his waist, and he was throwing his dick into me like he was trying to fit a piece in.

"Fuuuuuuck. Mmmmmm," he growled.

"Shit." I was tightly wrapped around him, and I felt his veins pulsing, so I knew he was cumming.

"You felt just like I knew you would." He kissed me and laid me down.

"Same." I giggled.

"I ain't tryna rush you, Passion." He kissed me.

"Good, because you scary, and I don't wanna be caught up again." I looked at him.

He responded with a kiss.

"I ain't scary." He laughed.

"You are," I said as he slipped his tongue into my mouth and kissed me until I was weak.

"What's scary about that?"

I was twerking with my tongue out in my mind.

"I hope I can get some breakfast in the morning." He picked up the remote and turned the TV on.

"Nigga, you kiddin' me? Shit, you can get breakfast, lunch, and dinner after that shit."

We both laughed, and it didn't take long to start up again.

While True slept, I felt some sense of guilt rush over me, but I had to put that shit aside because I had to go on, even if he was just a dream. I knew I couldn't nail a guy like True down, but I guess I could enjoy the ride until he got tired of me too. I got under him, and he wrapped his arm around me and kissed my lips.

"Go to sleep," he said and began snoring again.

I smiled and fell asleep too.

"THIS LIL MUTHAFUCKA RIGHT HERE?" I pointed at the scrawny ass Snoop Dog looking motherfucker in front of me.

"Yeah, bitch, a scrawny nigga got ya shit, though. You need to be mad at yourself and these week ass bitches you got handling shit." He laughed, but I smacked him in the mouth with a wrench.

We were sitting on the docks of an abandoned seafood warehouse. His mouth poured blood as he sat tied up and swinging from a chair.

"We found the work, Brady. Right, that's your name?" I asked.

"Fuck you, bitch," he said and spit a tooth, but he would spit more.

I smacked him again in the mouth with the wrench.

"He pussy, dump his ass," Pashia said.

"Drop him." I looked at Carsell.

She nodded and pushed him over the water.

"Y'all can't kill me." He laughed.

"Watch us."

I took out a lighter and the gasoline then began to toss it on him. He looked terrified as he acted like he could get out those cuffs. All four legs and arms were locked in.

"Bitch—" I threw the match and watched him burst into flames.

"Arrrggghhh! Arrrggghhhhh. Nooooo." He screamed as his flesh burned.

I could hear his skin crisping. I let him burn for five minutes alive, and then we dropped him in the water with the cement blocks.

"Bitch ass." Pashia looked down into the water.

"Aight, lets get the fuck outta here," I said to her.

I rode with Pashia, so we got into her car and peeled out.

"I'm glad we found that shit," I said.

My father had called, even though I hadn't told him. I found it before he could be upset.

"Yeah, we good, just need to tighten up. These niggas think we sweet, but we gon' show they ass better than we can tell them."

"Fuck yeah, bitch. I been meaning to tell your ass some shit," I said.

"Ohhh, bitch, what?" She perked up.

"I fucked True."

"Ooooohh, bitch, when?" she screamed.

"Last week." I smiled.

"Y'all been talkin'?" she asked.

"Some texts, but I don't wanna get deep. That's Chino's cousin. Plus, he's a man hoe," I explained.

"Well, yeah, he a man hoe, but fuck Chino. Don't let him be a reason."

"Girl, that nigga stroke ain't no joke. I see how a bitch could be dickmatized." I giggled.

"You nasty." She pushed me. "Well, I for one am happy for you."

"Thanks, bitch." I smiled.

"Look at you smilin' and shit. Girl, your ass in love already," she said.

"Nah, I got a date with somebody else tonight. I'm exploring my options." I stuck my tongue out."

"Bitch out here wildin'." She snapped.

"Yes, ma'am." I did the duck lips.

"Biiiitch." She laughed.

I had agreed to go out with this guy I met at the mall. His name was Calvin. He was cool and all, but, of course, all I could think about was True when I spoke to him the last few times.

"Well, we can do a double date if you want. I can get Lucci or Fitz out." She shrugged.

"Bitch, who is Fitz?" I asked.

"Oh, I ain't tell you about Fitz. He's my lil boo. You know me and Lucci serious but not official, so I got options too, hoe." She smirked.

"Aight cool, it's tonight eight at Peter Lugar," I told her.

"Okay cool. We almost to your spot," she said, looking out the window.

"I gotta go see what I can throw together," I told her.

"Me too, let's wear something yellow together."

"Yaasss, I got yellow." I nodded.

"Aight, cool. See you tonight." We hugged, and I got out.

I made it up to my place and rushed in so I could smoke and chill for the next two hours. My phone was on do not disturb, so I looked and saw a text from True, Chino, and my mother.

True: Wyd? Still hiding from me?

Me: Lol, I ain't hiding from you.

True: Then let me come thru. You owe me more breakfast.

I smiled so hard. Dammit, I had this date.

Me: When I get home. I'm going out in a few.

True: Fuck you goin?

I snapped my neck like he could see me.

Me: BOOOOOOYYYYYYY.

True: I'ma see yo ass later.

Me: lol aight.

True: Laugh now, shorty

That shit sent a shockwave to the twat.

I grabbed a yellow mini dress with my diamond earrings and matching bracelet. I put on some black red bottom platforms then fixed up my make up and sprayed some Halle berry on.

"Yes, bitch, yeessss." I snapped pictures in the mirror.

I saw that Chino's ass texted me again when I didn't respond. I didn't even see what he said.

Bitchass: *The fuck you doin'? Why you not answering the phone?*

Me: *Cuz, nigga I don't want to. The fuck. I ain't ya girl no more nigga.*

Bitchass: *you always gon be my girl, fuck you mean.*

I ignored that shit and heard the concierge bell going off.

"Yes." I hit the digital screen, and Emily's face popped up.

"Hi, we have a gentleman here to see you. Calvin Bradshaw." She smiled.

"Okay, I'll be down."

I grabbed my small clutch and put my ID and one of my bank cards in it.

I texted Pashia that we were on the way then I looked at myself one more time and left. After hitting my floor on the elevator, I got nervous. Yeah, I hit True off, but I haven't been on a real date with nobody but Chino's ass.

Once I got off the elevator, I smiled at Calvin, who looked like Morris Chestnut in his *Boyz in the Hood* days.

"Damn, baby girl, you came to make me stop breathing." He held his chest.

"Thank you." I smiled at his compliment.

"Nah, thank you," he said as we walked outside.

He pulled open the door to a double parked Skyline, and I was loving it. It was a sexy ass car. I slid in, and he hopped around to the other side and secured himself.

"I'm the luckiest nigga in New York right now," he said.

"You got mad game, I see." I laughed.

"No game. You must ain't see yourself tonight." He looked at my thighs.

"Drive, dude." I giggled.

He pulled off, and my phone started ringing. I saw it was Pashia.

"Hey, sis."

"Hey, we at the spot already, but bitch, you gon' wild out," she said.

My phone cut off, and I saw that my battery had died.

"Shit," I said.

"What's wrong?" he asked.

"That was my cousin, the one I texted you was meeting us," I said.

"Oh okay. Something wrong?" He looked over.

"I don't know. My phone died before I could hear. I'm sure everything's cool."

The way she sounded, some shit was wrong.

We pulled into the parking lot and got a ticket from the

attendant then we were arm in arm walking through the front door.

"We're meeting someone. I see them," I told the hostess.

"Sure." She waved us through.

I saw Pashia and Lucci from the side, but when I walked around the wall, True and that girl Vee sat there as well.

"Shit," I said under my breath.

"You okay?" Calvin asked.

"Yeah, I see my cousin," I told him and went to the table.

True looked at me and nodded.

"Hey, cuz," I said with my eyes large. She raised her eyebrows.

"This is Calvin. Calvin, this is my cousin, Pashia, and her... Lucci, and True and Vee," I said feeling True burn a hole through my ass.

"Nice to meet y'all," Calvin said.

"You too." Pashia shook his hand.

Calvin pulled my chair out, and he took a seat next to me.

"So, did y'all order any appetizers?" I tried hard not to look at this nigga True.

"Yes, and they should be coming. I'm starving," Pashia said.

"Shit, I just want a steak. But I'ma fuck it all up," Lucci said.

"So, how y'all meet up?" True asked Calvin.

"I saw shorty in the mall and shit. She was fine as hell, and you know I had to holla." Calvin shrugged.

"Oh, yeah. That's wassup." He nodded.

Vee was giving his ass a death stare.

"I like that dress, Passion, but True don't like me to dress all stank like that. No offense," Vee said.

"Bitch, what? Stank, where? It's a mini dress, but won't you worry about what your husband wanna see you in, hoe?" I spat.

Her mouth hung open, and True had a little smirk on his face.

"Bitch, you don't know shit about my business," she snapped.

"Girl, who blood you talkin' to?" Pashia jumped in.

"Look, y'all ain't boutta fuck up this steak, cuz I'm hungry, and y'all doin' too much," Lucci said.

"You good, shorty?" Calvin looked at me and rubbed the back of my neck.

"Yeah." I squinted at True.

"Here's the drinks." The waitress came back and looked at me and Calvin with a smile.

"Hi, I'm Samantha. I'll take your drink orders." She continued smiling at me and Calvin.

"Thanks, I have a long island, strong as hell," I said.

Everybody laughed, even Vee's simple ass.

"I'll take a cognac," Calvin said.

"Umm, I'll have a long island too," Vee said.

"And I'll take some Remy. This soda was flat, babes," Pashia said after sipping from her cup.

"Okay, be right back with your drink and appetizers." Samantha smiled.

"I'm sorry," Vee said to me.

"It's cool." I looked at the menu.

We all had small talk, but I was feeling jealous as hell watching Vee smile all in True's face. My body began to tremble when I thought about the sex we had.

"Cuz, run to the bathroom with me." Pashia got up.

"Okay." I was about to stand up when Calvin got up and pulled my chair out.

"Thanks." I kissed his cheek and was sure to make this ass move when I walked.

"I'ma hurt you," I said to Pashia as we walked.

"Bitch, Lucci stupid ass was at his spot when I called to tell him the move. He said the shit to True, and here we are." She pushed the bathroom door open.

"Girl, that bitch tried it."

"Honey, did she? Bitch was pissed. Got on my nerves the whole time we been waiting for y'all." Pashia went in the stall.

"Girl, he tryna make me jealous." I took out my phone and texted him.

Me: Really?

"Well, are you?" she asked.

"No," I lied.

"Lies. You look like the grinch all green over there."

"Bitch, please." I applied some moisturizer for this 24-hour matte.

"Girl, you need to stop playing and snatch his ass up, chile." She washed her hands.

"Girl, so he can Chino my ass? No ma'am."

We walked out the bathroom, and Vee walked by. We continued to the table, and I noticed that Calvin was gone.

"Where Calvin go?" I asked.

"He said he had to go grab something out the car," Lucci said.

My phone vibrated, and I bit down on my bottom lip.

True: you look too good in that dress to waste it on a lame, shorty. Been thinkin' bout that pussy. I'ma have to taste it next time.

I smiled and locked my phone. I looked up, and True was smirking.

"Finally, damn."

The waitress set two plates of bacon down and jumbo shrimp cocktails.

We gave her the entrée orders then we started crushing the bacon. I was glad they thought about us and got three shrimp cock tails.

"Don't y'all think Maccina is a cute name for a girl?" Vee burst out of nowhere.

"I don't like it." Pashia shrugged.

"I just can't think of what we gon' name the baby." She smirked at me.

"You pregnant?" I asked.

"Yeah, True didn't tell y'all?" She shoved him.

He looked apologetically at me, but I just shrugged it off. He wasn't my nigga.

"Congrats," I said.

Calvin reached under the table and touched my thigh. I looked at him like he was crazy, and he removed it.

"My bad," he said in a low whisper.

After we ate, I was ready to go the hell home. The more Calvin drank, the more irritating his ass became. He was laughing loudly and embarrassing us.

"I'm ready." I got up, and he tried to pull the chair out again but fell on his face.

"Aye, that nigga funny as hell." True laughed.

"Fuck you, True," I said as I helped Calvin up.

"Later, I gotta drop shorty off then we can talk." He got up.

"For real, nigga?" Vee screamed and stormed out.

"Y'all ghetto ass mufuckas." Pashia got up.

"Let's go." I yelled at Calvin.

"I'm coming, baby girl." He laughed and fell back down.

I was humiliated, so I rushed out the restaurant then stood in the street to hail a cab. Once one pulled up, I jumped in.

I read my address off to him, and he pulled off. I couldn't get my ass home fast enough. I swiped my card through the attached pad on the divider.

"Thanks." I hopped out and rushed into my building.

Once I got up to my door, I opened it and threw my bag on my couch then kicked my shoes off.

"Simple fucker," I said, thinking of Calvin.

I picked up a blunt I was smoking earlier and stripped down ass hole naked and sparked up.

Motor sport, put that thing in sport.

My ringtone sounded, and I rolled my eyes when I saw True calling.

"What?" I answered.

"Shorty, fuck all that attitude. Where you at?" True asked.

"At home about to go to bed," I said with attitude. He could have said he had a baby on the way.

"Nah, stay up. I'ma be there in a minute. I'm sorry I ain't let you know, ma." He hung up.

His ass never gave me a chance to even respond.

I quickly ran around and put shit away so it could be spotless.

I grabbed my Kimono robe and my slippers.

Knock, knock

I took a deep breath and went to the door. I swung it open, and True stood there with a bottle of Moet and some strawberries.

"You lucky I knocked this time," he said and quickly attacked my mouth as he slammed the door behind him.

"So, you boutta have a kid, huh?" I folded my arms.

"I mean, if it means anything, it was before—" He stopped.

"Before what?"

"I started to like you, aight? Like feeling you mad hard."

He touched my face and kissed me. "You looked good as fuck tonight." He kissed on my neck and laid me on the couch.

"You too." I grabbed his head as he sucked on my neck. I let the shit go and allowed all this to happen.

"Fuck." I moaned as he slid his fingers into my pussy.

"You soaked." True kissed me passionately like he loved me. Then he dropped down and pushed his tongue deep inside of me.

"Oh, God." I moaned.

It had only been seconds but the way he was on my clit made me wanna cum hard as hell already.

"Sugarwalls," he whispered and slurped on my pussy like he was eating a funnel cake with strawberries.

"I'ma cum, True." I started shaking and felt myself explode all on his face.

He chuckled and used his shirt to wipe it off.

Bang, Bang, Bang.

"Passion!" I heard Chino at the door.

How the fuck he get through the front desk?

"Shit, True," I said in a panic.

"Man, fuck him," he barked and positioned himself over top of me.

"True, I'ma be too loud." I moaned as he pushed inside of me raw.

"Fuuuuuck." I screamed.

"Bitch, you fuckin' a nigga in there?" I heard Chino yelling and kicking the door.

"Shit juicy." True slipped his tongue into my mouth.

"Mmmmm, oh my God." I was ready to cum.

"I'ma kill that nigga!" Chino continued to bang for like five minutes until I heard what sounded like police radios.

"Sit on my lap." True got up, completely ignoring his cousin possibly getting locked up.

"Yes, True," I said, remembering the last time.

"Shit, say that again." He slid me down on his dick.

"YES, TRUE!" I screamed, feeling his dick hit that back wall.

"Aye shorty, I swear." He gripped my waist and held on as I slapped down hard, I saw his legs jumping, so I knew I was giving it to his ass right.

He grabbed my titties, held me tight, and began grunting like he was cumming.

"Nigga, I know you ain't nut in me," I said out of breath.

"I had to." He laughed.

"Oh my God, now I gotta shame walk to the drug store." I shook my head.

I felt like a nasty hoe. I hadn't known True long enough to have unprotected sex, shit sex at all, but we were grown on that aspect. But what if he had something I started to panic.

"You straight as far as health, right? I'm nervous. HIV is real." I felt my chest cave in with fear.

"Aye, don't fuckin' disrespect me like that. I ain't never been no drip dick ass nigga, shorty. You got me confused," he said and pulling me off him.

"I'm just sayin', shit." I walked to the back to pee.

"Aye, you got that jacuzzi joint, huh. Let's do this in there. We can flip that TV and shit on," he said, following me into the bathroom.

"Okay, ohh that 600 pound life jawn on my DVR," I said.

I don't know why I looked at that show. Them people pissed me off half the time.

"Hell naw, I watched that shit one time. When that fat, crooked mouth bitch kept saying, 'do you believe in God, doctor?' I wanted to slap her and her goofy ass nigga," he said serious as hell, but I laughed.

"Nah, for real. I be rootin' for them when they lose weight and shit, but when they just choose to die, shit irritates me." He now laughed himself.

We walked out the bathroom and headed to my jacuzzi room, which looked like a luxury bathroom without a toilet. There was an open shower, but the middle was a large, rectangular Jacuzzi, and I had three flat screens on three of the walls.

I grabbed the remote, and True set the strawberries and Moet on the side. I hit the heater, and we slid in. I turned the TV on Sanford and son. I still liked the classics. Chino would always make fun of me so much that I wouldn't turn it on when he was around.

"Damn, I be lookin' at this shit too. This and the Jeffersons," True said.

Oh my God, please stop having so much in common with me.

"You don't know shit about no Jeffersons," I teased as he poured our glasses.

"I'm older than you. Your young ass don't know shit about it." He picked up a strawberry and dropped it in my glass.

"What the hell we doin'?" I asked and looked at the TV.

"I don't know, but it feels good to me." He kissed me.

"You say that to all them hoes." I smirked.

"Nah. Not at all, lil shorty." He laughed.

"You spendin' the night?" I asked.

"You should know that already."

He kissed me again, and we started talking again and getting to know each other a little better. We ended up mind fucking each other then actually fucking each other. The more I learned, the more I wanted.

CHINO

I sat outside of Passion's spot hoping to see what fuck nigga was in there smashing my bitch. I was gon' put two in the nigga's head. I waited all night, but the only people who came out was corny ass white mufuckas. I knew she wasn't fucking none of them. I couldn't believe I really lost her ass for good. I slammed my head on the head rest. Passion was driving me crazy. She really left me.

Fuck it. I pulled off and called Cherry.

"What, Chino?" she said in a nasty tone.

"I want you to move up here with lil Ronnie," I said.

"What?" she asked in surprise.

"Mmm, what happened? Passion ain't take ya ass back?" she spoke sarcastically.

"Bitch, see, I try to be nice to your ass."

"Okay, Chino. You got a place?" she asked.

"Yeah, I got a spot. We can finally be together now," I said, not really giving a fuck about being with her.

"Well, come get us. We can get a truck," she said excitedly.

"Nah, you don't need shit. I'ma get us all new shit. My cousin putting me on."

"Okay, well shoot, I can ride up there now if that's the case." She sounded like she was getting up.

"Aight, I'ma send you the new address," I told her.

"Okay." She hung up.

Fuck it, I would move on with Cherry ass. That bitch, Passion wanted to play games, so I was gon' rub the shit in.

I got to the two bedroom I had purchased through True's realtor about eight blocks from Passion when I thought I had a fucking chance of winning her back. I called to see if he was still having that lil get together this weekend. I pulled off but stopped when I heard the sirens from a passing fire truck

"Wassup, bro?" I heard, but I could hear the same truck in the background of his phone.

I looked around because that would have been a coincidence like a motherfucker. I brushed the shit off.

"I was about to hit you to see if ya ass was still havin' that get together," I said.

"Yeah, it's going down," he replied.

"Aight, cool. I'ma have Cherry with me. You think ya moms will watch Ronnie for us?" I asked.

"Probably. Ask her."

"Aight, I'ma holla at you later."

"Wait, you need to come through later," he said.

"What's wrong?"

"Why some shit gotta be wrong?" he asked.

"Aight, nigga." I hung up. I hoped he hadn't found out I was triple cutting that shit I had down in Philly.

I turned up my music and headed to my new home. That shit left a feeling in my gut about when I called True, but the nigga wouldn't go behind my back and do no shit like that. That shit fucked up my mind the rest of the day. I would go crazy for Passion, and the thought of any nigga touching her made my fuckin' blood boil, but for it to be my cousin. I don't know what the fuck I would do.

Cherry had called me once I got home and said she was just getting on the road and shit. I knew traffic was probably fucked up, so it would take like five hours for real. Since it was gonna be late, I decided to go to the grocery store and grab food and some other shit that I needed to have on deck. I should have hit her ass when I had shit right.

I needed beds and some more shit. I just got the keys yesterday and slept on a futon and shit. When I passed this furniture spot, I turned around so I could check shit out real quick since I had food in the trunk. Being a dude, I knew I wasn't about to be in there all day, I quickly picked out a boy's bedroom race car set and a cherrywood bedroom set for us. I also picked out a dining and living room set. All in under thirty minutes. I didn't understand what took bitches so long.

"We can deliver it this evening for an extra four hundred," Farlin, the associate who helped me said.

"Aight, cool."

I paid for everything and then left so I could get back.

My phone began to ring, and I saw Passion calling. That shit made me stop everything.

"Hello." I picked up happier than hell.

"Shiiiit." I heard her screaming then slapping noises.

"Bitch!" I yelled and hung up.

I threw my phone and cracked the screen.

"Fuck!" I yelled as I kicked the phone.

I jumped in the car, grabbed my burner cell, and set it in my lap. I drove home pissed off and determined to say fuck Passion stupid ass.

I called Cherry on the burner cell to let her know to call that one now. She said they were in heavy traffic, just as I thought, I should have just flown them out. Now that I about it, ain't no sense in chasing a bitch that didn't wanna fuck with me. It was gon' fuck me up, but I had to say fuck her and keep the shit pushing. I looked at the picture of Passion that I kept on the dash and threw it out the window.

"IT FEELS good waking up in a new place." Cherry smiled as she got up.

"Yeah, this bed is off the hook too." I got up.

I looked at the clock and saw that it was after eight. True

never got a chance to meet up with me, so I was gonna go holla at him today.

"I can't believe we moved up here. I always wanted to live in New York," she said.

"Well, here you are." I kissed her.

"And what part we in again?" she asked.

"Brooklyn." I got up.

"This gon' be fun. I'ma get friends and be like them white bitches from *Sex in the City*." She giggled.

"Yeah, okay." I grabbed my towel and got ready to get in the shower.

"Why I got a feeling you not really happy I'm here?" Cherry walked up.

"Look, man, don't start shit wit' me. Man, I got you and my son here because I want y'all to be here. Stop lookin' for trouble and shit, man," I said, knowing I was lying.

"Aight, Chino." She tried to walk past, but I pulled her to my chest and slowly kissed her.

I just wanted her to shut up because I knew she would carry on.

"Are you still giving me money to go shopping today?" she asked when I let her go.

"Yeah, make sure you get a lot of clothes and not just a bunch of expensive nothing," I warned as I handed over my Capital One card.

"I am." She tucked it in her bra.

"Oh, and see if you can get some comforters and shit," I told her while turning the shower on.

"Aight." She walked off.

I quickly got showered and dressed.

"Daddy." Ronnie ran in the room when I was leaving out.

"What's up, man?" I rubbed the top of his head.

He could never call me daddy when Passion was around. The time he slipped is when Cherry stopped bringing him around.

"I wanna go," he said, not knowing where the hell I was going.

"Daddy will take you somewhere when I get back." I walked him downstairs where Cherry was cooking breakfast.

"You gon' eat?" she asked.

"No. Be right back." I hugged Ronnie and rolled out.

A second later, right after pulling off, I got a text from Cherry's ass, crying about me not kissing her bye and shit. She wanted to be a wife so bad, but to me, the bitch wasn't that type of bitch yet. I ain't even reply to her ass. I didn't even know where the fuck I was supposed to meet True ass at. He always moving around and shit.

I called him, but his phone went straight to voicemail.

"What the fuck?" I tried again but the same shit.

I decided to drive to his loft where he spent most of his time. When I pulled up, I saw Lucci getting out of his whip, and knew I was in the right place.

"Wassup?" I said when I hopped out.

"Ain't shit," he said.

"You ready?" he asked.

"What you mean?" I asked.

All of a sudden, niggas came out from everywhere with guns drawn. They were all True's New Freezer niggas which I could tell because of the chain.

"Put him in," I heard True say, and a bag went over my head.

"What the fuck?"

I started swinging, but I started getting hit and then lifted up. I was thrown in what I was sure was a trunk once I heard it slam.

"We blood, nigga. You fucked up," I said as I kicked.

I pulled the bag off my head as we pulled off. Then, I used the light of my cell phone to look for the pull string for the trunk, which was cut off. I realized this nigga was tryna get rid of me to get Passion. I knew I wasn't tripping. It was cool because they better be ready when they open this motherfucking trunk. I was about to go all the fuck out.

We drove for a long ass time, and then we abruptly stopped. I felt the car shifting and shit like niggas was getting out, so I got ready to jump out. The trunk unlocked and popped open. It was quiet as hell. I slowly opened the trunk and saw that I was alone. I hopped out the trunk and turned around to see the niggas behind me with True and Lucci standing in front.

"What the fuck is this?" I said, throwing up my hands and ready for whatever.

"Nigga, you can't beat us all, so go ahead and put ya

hands down." True chuckled.

"So, what's good, nigga? I don't give a fuck how man—"

"Shut the fuck up," True said as he walked up. "You said you wanted to be New freezer, mufucka," he barked.

"Okay, but you could have told me." I still tried to tell the nigga why I was heated.

"Nigga, you in or out? I ain't gon' ask again. You still whining and shit like a bitch, and it makes me think you ain't with the shit," True said.

"Yeah, I'm in."

"Good." He pushed a .9 into my hands.

"The fuck is this?" I asked.

"If you can survive for an hour with no hits, you in." He smirked.

"What you mean?" I asked.

"Nigga, you need to run."

He backed up, and a shot rang out. I looked around and saw niggas with the straps on me.

"Are you fuckin' crazy?" I said, but the shots kept coming, and I sped off into the woods.

What the fuck kind of initiation is this shit? I thought as I went behind a big as tree and breathed heavily.

I looked in the clip and saw it was full. I could hear footsteps coming toward me, and I kept thinking that maybe this was his way of killing me. *Did he find out about Gia?* I took a deep breath then jumped out and started shooting. I hit two niggas, and they dropped, then I ran off.

"Fuck." I heard one of them say.

I didn't know how long I was in them woods, but I came out a New Freezer Boy. I saw the niggas I shot, and they were straight. Come to find out, it was rubber bullets and shit.

"You wild." I dapped True up after grabbing my new chain.

"Yeah, well, I wanted you think you really had to defend yourself, and I had to see how you got down. You my cuz and I fuck with you, but I only keep real hittas, you feel me? Shit is real out here."

"Thanks, bruh. So, what's my setup?" I asked.

"You gon' be working with Flight in the gardens. We got a floor setup over there, and you can be a lieutenant. Keep them niggas in line. Flight is your right hand. Oh, and before it's an issue, Passion got some shit set up over there too," he said.

"Fuck, Passion. I'm on money moves. You feel me?" I told him, lying like I wasn't hurt over her ass.

"Aight, cuz all that emotional shit ain't gon' fly, so just letting you know. But fuck all that, we havin' a celebration tonight.

"Bet!" I said and got in the car with him and Lucci.

I looked down at my chain and couldn't believe I thought my cousin was about to be on some foul shit. I felt fucked up about the thought, but you never know sometimes. Shit, now I was ready to party.

A FEW HOURS LATER, I found myself arguing and shit instead of enjoying the get together. I was on the phone with this nagging ass bitch.

"Bitch, I said I was coming back when the fuck I'm done," I yelled at Cherry, who was blowing my whole fucking life right now.

"Nigga, you ain't been back since this morning."

"I know. I been busy," I said as the bitch Nina twerked on my dick.

True had the hook up with the baddest bitches, and I was gon' enjoy this new freezer lifestyle.

"Come on, daddy," Nina cooed.

"Who the fuck is that, Chino?" Cherry screamed before I hung up.

"Nigga, these bitches bad," I told True as Nina tugged on me.

"Fuck yeah, and I get all the hoes who come through here tested before they get here. We like clean pussy around here." True chuckled as he rubbed the ass of some thick ass shorty on his lap.

"Where we goin' girl?" I asked the bitch, Nina, as we walked off.

"To the moon."

She giggled and pulled me inside a small room off the side of the kitchen. I realized it was a laundry room when she hit the lamp. I smiled hard when I saw the other bitch sitting on top of the dryer.

"Come here."

Her sexy, cinnamon ass pulled on me, and I landed right between her legs on the dryer. She slowly kissed me as Nina pulled my jeans down.

"I wanna see a freak show." I pulled back and pulled shorty's G-string off.

"Oh, you a nasty boy," Nina said. She was on her knees between the chick's legs licking on her pussy. She must have been doing a hell of a job because ole girl was going crazy.

"Stand up," I told Nina, and she did without taking her mouth off the pussy. I leaned down and grabbed the condom out my jeans then rolled it on.

"Y'all bad as fuck," I said as I slid into Nina.

"Shit, this nigga's dick big as fuck, sis," Nina screamed as I pounded.

"Well, hurry up and let me get some," the bitch on the dryer said.

The way Nina was throwing it, I was ready cum, so I pulled out and smacked her on the ass. I really wanted to feel this hoe. The way Nina was eating the pussy, I wanted to lick the shit myself. I pulled her to the edge of the dryer and licked her juicy ass pussy. She was soaked from being ate out, but I was about to make the bitch cum.

"Fuck." She grabbed the back of my head. She tasted sweet as fuck too.

"Cum, hoe." I slurped and licked on her clit, and she started jumping then I felt her squirting all in my face. I grabbed a folded towel off the rack and wiped my face.

"Come on," she begged and grabbed my dick.

I grabbed her neck and roughly pushed into her tight pussy.

"Oh shit," I said, loving the way she felt. She felt better than Nina, and her pussy was tighter.

"Yes, daddy!" she cried as I murdered her pussy.

I tried to go in the bitch's kidney the way I was dogging her ass. I pulled out and took the condom off. I had to feel this bitch raw.

"Shit," she squealed as I picked her up and put her on the wall. She wrapped her legs around me, and I felt like I was making love to this bitch.

"Damn, well y'all don't need me, I see," Nina said and left.

"What's your name?" I asked, feeling like I was ready to cum.

"Jamina." She threw her head back and began to cum. I let it go too.

"You on birth control?" I asked.

"Yeah." She was breathing heavily.

"I want your number," I said after pulling my pants up.

"Okay." She blushed.

I called her phone and told her to save me after giving her my name. I had to get back up with this bitch again. it was something about her that had a nigga wanting some more of that shit.

My phone began to ring, and I saw it was Cherry calling me again.

"What?" I screamed.

"I'm lea—" I hung up and went back to the party.

This was my new life right here.

2 WEEKS *later*

Cherry was fast asleep after I gave her some dick to shut the bitch up. She will blow your whole life the way she cries like she was some stand up bitch, when she was only there because she fucked her friend's nigga.

I went to the backyard and lit up a blunt before calling Jamina. I had been fucking her since the party, and I had started to like her a little bit.

"So, what you doin'?" I asked, wishing I could go get some of that shit like now.

"Nothing, I just watched *Girls Trip*, and ready to lay down." She yawned.

"You miss a nigga?" I asked.

"No, we ain't there yet." She giggled.

"Chino!" Cherry screamed behind my head.

"Fuck!" I yelled. She scared the fuck out of me.

"Who the fuck is that?" Cherry came toward me and snatched my phone.

"Hello," she yelled. "Bitch, why the fuck you on the phone with my nigga?" Cherry continued, but I guess she got hung up on.

"What? It don't feel good to have your nigga cheating

and shit? You did it to Passion, and now you all hurt." I laughed and went in the house.

"So, why the fuck you even ask me up here?" she cried behind me.

"Because, I want to take care of you and my son."

I went in the drawer then grabbed a shirt and some jeans. Then I took my shoes and some soap and put it in the bag.

"Where the fuck you goin'?" she pushed me.

"Since you know about the bitch now, I ain't gotta hide shit. I'ma go fuck with her and see you tomorrow." I kissed her cheek and walked out.

I called shorty back. She was mad, but let me come through anyway. I was about to be hooked on her pussy. Shit, she might be my next bitch.

PASSION

"*D*id y'all take care of them niggas who tried to run down on y'all?" True asked, holding me after another session of fucking.

I hated that a I had real feelings for him because he wasn't playing with that bachelor life, and I knew I would be hurt. He was so good to me, and we were only having sex and chilling with each other. I knew we could be much more, but this was good too. It was safe for me.

"Yeah, I'm tired of these niggas tryna bitch us," I said and kissed him.

"Y'all doing it the right way. I done heard the Dirty Diamond Girls putting work in." He smiled.

"Shut up." I laughed.

"I like that name, though. That's why I got something for y'all," he said.

"What?" I jumped up excitedly.

True got up and ran out the room then came back in with a large, gold box.

"You tryna spoil me, man." I smiled.

"Why not?" He smirked.

I opened it and covered my mouth.

"You said you would be queen, and you are."

He kissed me and put the crown on my head, which contained a large diamond in the middle.

"Now, I know you can't wear that at all times, so I thought this was fitting for every day." He took the chain that had a large diamond shape with diamonds filled in. The tip of the diamond contained a crown.

"And all the other girls wear this." He showed me the ones that matched mine, but without the crown.

"You had to pay a grip for this." I shook my head.

"Yeah, me and the niggas put up for y'all. I mean, seeing as thought most of them bitches fucking with somebody from my crew."

"True." I laughed.

"So, I was thinking about flying out to Cozumel in a month or so." He grabbed my hand.

"That's Mexico, right?" I asked. "What you doing out there?"

"Taking you on vacation." He kissed my neck.

"You want me to go on vacation with you?" I beamed.

"Duh, why else would I let you know."

"I thought we was just friends with benefits." I turned my lip up.

"Girl, shut up. You know I like your ass." He pulled me on top of him.

"You only like my ass?" I teased.

"I like that too, but I like you, period."

I felt his dick rising and bit my bottom lip.

"Nigga, I'm already sore because of you. I should kick your ass for running off my date last night." I punched him.

I was gonna go out with Calvin again, but when we got out front, True had twenty niggas out there waiting.

"When I say I wanna come through, I mean it."

I felt him rubbing the head of his dick against my opening, and he pulled me down on it with a hard stroke.

"You ain't my nigga." I closed my eyes and enjoyed how he was fucking me. Even on top of him, he had control.

"You want me to be?" He pulled my face closer to his and slowly slid his tongue into my mouth. "Shit, you might be having my baby too." He pulled back.

"You crazy." I moaned as he flipped me over.

"You ain't ready yet anyway." He cuffed my leg and sent me into shocks.

"Fuck, fuck, fuck." I beat on his back, but that ain't stop him.

He came deep inside of me, and I was still cumming.

"Your ass gon' be in a wheelchair."

He got up after kissing me and turned on my shower. I had gotten so comfortable with him. We spent the night over each other's house at least four times a week. I needed to just tell the nigga I was his, but I still felt like it would be rushing it.

"So, I'm having some shit at the spot. Chino might there, but you know you always welcome wherever I'm at." He stood ass naked with a towel over his shoulder.

"You had to bring him in." I rolled my eyes.

"At the end of the day, he's still blood. My cuz a real street soldier, and he's beneficial to my organization," he said.

He let me know that Chino was a New Freezer Boy now. I felt sick because I would probably have to see his ass more than I wanted to.

"I feel you. Just keep him away from my ass." I laughed.

I honestly felt like I had let Chino go, I felt so much happier without all that stress and shit.

"I got you, ma. Now come get in this shower with me." He used his finger to beckon me.

"You ain't gonna kill me."

I got up and went my ass right in there.

"I LIKE THIS, TRUE."

I smiled as we walked through King of Prussia, and my eyes landed on this nice ass two piece. Even though we weren't going on our trip for a while, he wanted to take me shopping for it.

"That's sexy as hell, shorty. Let's get it." He pulled me into the store with me giggling behind him.

A man was playing a large, white piano in the middle of the mall floor. They were giving the piano away.

"I always wanted to learn how to play." I smiled.

"Then why don't you get some lessons?" True replied.

"You so supportive." I giggled.

"You supposed to be." He kissed me.

"True." We both turned and saw his cousin Medina walking up. "Hey, Passion." She smiled.

"Wassup, blood?" True hugged her.

"So, y'all up here together?"

"I was just—"

"I ain't trippin', I mean y'all grown." She shrugged. "But Chino ain't gon' be so understanding."

"Man, you let me handle Chino. Mind ya business." True play slapped her.

"Whatever, so you know I'm up here with your mother and Queen, right?" she said and turned around.

"There they go! Auntie!" she screamed like a lunatic.

"My baby."

I got stuck when I saw the woman. She looked so much like Abbie. I assumed the girl was True's sister since she looked like her.

"How you doin', sweetheart?" She looked at me strangely like I looked at her.

"I didn't know Abbie had a twin," I said, still taken aback.

"Wait, ain't you passion fruit or some shit? Chino's bitch." The girl snapped her finger, breaking the silence.

"It's Passion, and I'm Chino's ex, yes," I said.

"Wait. True, what the hell?" his mom said.

"Can I grab my son for a minute?" She pulled True aside.

"Thanks, Medina," I said to her.

"So, you fuckin' my bro, now? Fuck, you tryna make it through the family?" The girl laughed.

"Queen, shut the fuck up. Many dicks as you had, some of them niggas gotta be related." Medina cut her off, and I laughed.

"Whatever. I'm Queen, True sister." She reached her hand out to shake, and I did so reluctantly.

"I don't have no problem with you and my son fooling around, but I don't want it to be a problem with him and his cousin. You understand?" his mother said when she walked back up.

"I do." I nodded.

"Well, listen, we were all gonna go eat some lunch, so join us. I'm Gabbie." She grabbed my hand and walked off with me.

While we ate at the small Italian eatery, I could tell I had impressed True's mother. Once I told her about how I planned to study nursing, she became excited. True didn't tell me she was a charge nurse. Under the table, True held my hand and smiled at me the whole time. Whatever he was feeling, he needed to know I felt the same damn way.

After we ate and said our goodbyes, True stopped me before we got in the car.

"I knew it wasn't just me, shorty. Everybody loves you."

He pushed me on the car and kissed me like he loved me. His words confused me because it was like he was telling me he loved me.

"I love you too," I said but immediately took it back. "I mean, I loved her too, like—" He kissed me again.

"I knew what you meant." He smirked and let me into the car.

I felt like I went too far. It was deep, and this was what I was scared of.

"I UNDERSTAND, but I don't think I wanna go out with you again," I said to Calvin as I stood at my front door.

I mean, I ain't been wanting shit but True's company, and he had been giving me that attention too. His phone would be blowing up off the hook, and he still would make sure I was a priority whenever we got together.

"It's 'cause of that nigga who stopped our last date and basically the first one, right? I knew something was up with y'all."

"Kinda." I shrugged.

"Damn, well aight, ma. Thanks for letting me up." He reached out to hug me, and I gave him one.

"I came the fuck up here to check on you, but you

already planning your next dick appointment," I heard Chino say.

"Nigga, why the fuck they keep letting you up here?" I screamed. "Somebody getting fired."

"This the new nigga? You the new nigga, cuz?" Chino asked Calvin.

"Nigga, fuck you talkin' to?" Calving jumped bad, but Chino was badder.

In a flash, he pulled out the gun and started beating Calvin in the head with it.

"Stay the fuck away my bitch, nigga. That was you in here fuckin' her the other night, bitch," he yelled as he stomped on Calvin.

I smacked Chino, and he pushed me in the apartment then closed the door.

"Passion, you gave my pussy away?" he said wild eyes and threw the bag on the floor.

He was stumbling and shit.

"Nigga, this ain't your pus—"

Slap!

He hit me across the face like he lost his mufuckin' mind.

"Nigga." I hit his ass with a two piece, but he got me right back and sent me across the couch.

"You fuckin' crazy?" I screamed.

He got down into my face.

I could smell the liquor. It was heavy too.

"I'm crazy about you. I used to tell that bitch she

couldn't never get my stomach wet like you, shorty. She was always wanting to break us up, but I only loved you, ma. I swear. Let me stay, and we can get married and shit. I was fucking this bitch, Jamisha. I like her and everything, but when she tried to make strawberry waffles, the shit was trash. She ain't you."

He started crying real tears. I thought about everything, all the shit his bitch ass put me through, and I pushed him off me.

"I moved on. I can't be with you no more. You ain't shit but poison." I spit blood at him.

Chino gripped my neck and tried to kiss me, but I punched him the stomach and tried to run. He grabbed my foot, and I fell. Then he climbed on top of me and started pulling at my under wear.

"Chino, what the fuck you doin?" I screamed, hitting his back.

He pushed his fingers into me, and I started crying.

"The fuck you cryin' for? We done fucked a thousand times," he said.

"Yeah, when I wanted to," I cried.

"Fuck it, man." He got up and lay across the couch then fell asleep.

I went to the back, grabbed my gun, then went back and pressed the shit against his forehead. He was so out of it, he didn't budge.

Frustrated, I went in my room and grabbed my phone then set it down. I couldn't get True involved in our shit. I locked my room door and sat on my bed. It was almost 9:00 on a damn Saturday night, and I was trapped in my bedroom. I had been through Chino's idiot drunk moods before.

I smoked and made sure I had the secure lock through the floor of my room. I ain't wanna kill Chino's ass, but if he didn't get the fuck out my shit soon...

TRUE

It was Saturday night, and Vee was nagging me to take her ass somewhere, so I decided we could go to the movies. I got two tickets to see Insidious 2 on Fandango. I had been spending all my time with Passion, to be honest, and I felt like I was ready to see where we could head. Yeah, Vee was pregnant with my kid, she claimed, but I wanted Passion. Our trip was coming up, and I was gonna go ahead and throw myself out there and tell her she was gon' be my shorty.

"How I look? You didn't even say nothing about my outfit," Vee said as we walked toward the movie theatre.

"You look nice, ma," I said, looking at a text from this shorty, Tana, who I pull up on sometimes.

I had to quickly close it because she sent a picture of her titties. I loved her pierced nipples, and she knew how to make a nigga wanna slide through.

"You all distracted," Vee said.

"I ain't, but what's up with you? Did you tell the nigga?" I asked

"No, not yet," she said.

"Vee, you like really tryin' my patience. You know I fucks wit chu, but ma, you gotta keep shit a hunnit when you dealin' wit me. I'ma cut your ass off after tonight. Until you let the nigga know wassup, don't call me for shit. Not a good morning text or nuffin," I told her ass.

"True, you not even bein' fair," she whined.

"I been fair," I said.

I looked up and saw my sister crying on the ground at the feet of her boyfriend. She grabbed his leg, and he slapped her. I ran up and knocked his ass down.

"He didn't mean it, True." She pulled on me.

"What the fuck you mean? You out here on your knees in the street. The fuckin' street!"

"I shouldn't have gotten smart. I embarrassed him. I'm sorry, bae." She tried to shake the nigga awake.

"I swear, you actin' trash as fuck," I said to her.

"Fuck you, True," she spat.

"Nah, fuck you," I said right back to her ass.

That's why I told my mother I didn't get involved with her wild shit.

"Your sis crazy," Vee said, looking back.

"No crazier than your ass." I laughed, and she wrapped her arms around my waist.

"You know I love you, right, True?" She looked up at me.

"I know." I kissed her on the cheek, and she looked disappointed like she always did when I didn't say the shit back.

We watched the movie, and the whole time, Vee was rubbing on my dick. I wished it was less people so I could slide in that shit. Once we were done, I wasn't really hungry, so I grabbed Vee some food to take back to my spot.

"You know I'ma have to go home," she said.

"I know. But I'ma have to hit that before you leave."

I started rubbing on her as soon as I opened the front door to the loft. I never really liked people at my house, so I always brought females there, even Vee.

"Oh, shit, Lucci." I heard a bitch moaning to the left of me.

"Nigga," I said to Lucci, and him and the girl jumped.

"My bad, cuz. I ain't know you was coming back tonight," he said.

"It's cool, we gon' head upstairs then." I nodded.

Lucci was the only other mufucka with the key to this spot. I trusted him to the death.

"You just let niggas come fuck on hoes whenever," Vee complained.

"Girl, I'm boutta fuck on you too." I grabbed her up and laid her on the bed.

I could feel my phone vibrating in my pocket, so I gave it a quick look.

It was Passion. I quickly jumped off Vee and answered.

"What good?" I said into the phone.

"Hey, I need you to come quick. I didn't know who else to call right now cuz I'm gonna kill his ass. This your cousin, and I want you to come get him. He's straight trippin'," she said hyped up.

"Why the fuck he even there? You let him up?" I said coolly.

"No, why the fuck would I do that? Know what, fine. I'ma kill his ass then." She hung up.

"Fuck," I said, looking at Vee.

"I'ma holla ta chu later, ma." I kissed her and ducked out.

I called Passion back, and she answered.

"I'm on the way," I said angrily.

"Aight." She hung up.

Once I pulled up to the high rise, I double parked and hopped out. I took the elevator to the 17th floor and went to her door.

Passion swung the door open, and she had a black eye and a busted lip.

"What the fuck he hit you?" I touched her face.

"Yeah, he came in here all drunk, and I tried to get him out. He punched me and tried to rape me," she cried.

I moved her out the way and pulled Chino up.

"What the fuck? True, fuck you doin' here?" he said confused.

"Nigga, you hit her?" I grabbed him up, and he started to fight me, but he was fucked up drunk.

"Nigga, you don't hit no female, and you damn sure don't hurt her." I stole his ass, and he went back out.

"Did he touch you there?" I asked.

She shook her head, and I kissed her, not giving a fuck that Chino was out cold.

"I'm sorry. Look, I'ma take him outta here and then I'll be back." I held her face.

"Thanks, True." She looked at me with those eyes, and I almost lost it.

"You mine, shorty. I should have been made that shit official regardless of what the fuck you talkin' about. I ain't that nigga right there, and I refuse to be without your ass. You hear me?" I looked in her eyes.

"You mean that?" She sounded like she wouldn't breathe until I said it.

"I love you." I kissed her and broke it before I took her to the room while Chino was laid out on the sofa.

"I love you too, True. I love you so much." She threw her arms around my neck, and we kissed like we were the only niggas in there right now.

"I'm coming back. I want you to show me how much," I told her and bit down on my lip.

The effect she had on me sexually had my dick already hard.

"I can't believe we saying this to each other," she said as tears rode down her cheeks.

"I can." I helped Chino up, and he started to come to.

"The fuck happened?" he asked, looking at me and Passion.

"I knocked you the fuck out, nigga. Let's go," I said as he tried to reach for Passion, but I moved him.

She was mine now, and everything the nigga did to her, he did to me at that point. I would sit the nigga down and explain when he was sober, but right now, he was going the fuck home.

I knew he didn't live too far from Passion, so once I got him in the car, I drove to the building I took him to the other day when we handled some shit in the Gardens. I took his phone when I heard it ringing, and it read Cherry.

"Hello?" I picked up.

"Who dis?" she responded.

"True, Chino's cousin. I'm down here and need to know what number y'all in," I said.

"What happened? He okay?" she asked.

"Bitch, what unit you in so I can bring him the fuck up?" I said, not giving a fuck about no other questions.

"We in 827."

She hung up, and I helped him walk up to the building. I let the concierge know where we were going. She knew Chino's face, even though he was walking dead and let us go.

"Oh, my God. He drunk?" the chick, Cherry asked.

"I'm out." I ain't bother responding to her.

I walked out the building and hopped back in my ride to

go holla at Passion's ass. I wanted her to tell me she loved me all night while I was in the pussy. Shit, it was only right.

I LOOKED over the paperwork for the new development that I was now part owner of, thanks to Guy. The nigga's business smarts was off the hook, and he was gon' make me a clean money millionaire.

"You're lucky to have William guiding you," Mardosa said, shaking my hand after signing the papers.

He was Guy's mans up there, and I had been working with him since that trip to Philly.

"He knows." Guy laughed. Of course, I called him William during meetings and shit for his cover.

"Let's go eat." Guy tapped my back, and we got up to leave the office.

We ended up at the pier eating some of the best food I ever had. It was a hole in the wall burger joint.

"So, how's my daughter doing? I talk to her, but of course, she won't tell me shit since she got something to prove."

"She doing good. Got herself going, and she making a name," I said, holding back any problems she might have had.

"Oh really? And how long y'all gonna wait to tell me y'all been fuckin' around?" he asked straight faced.

"Damn, don't shit get by you, huh?" I drank down my beer.

"My daughter not some some pass around—" he started.

"Nah, she's definitely not. I love Passion, and I'ma love her like she never been loved by no nigga. And no offense, not even you."

He looked at me like I was crazy, and a slow smile crept across his face.

"I'm gon' hold you to that." He raised his beer, and we tapped them.

"I think my wife gotta crush on you. You might have her and Passion fighting." He chuckled.

"Ohh nah, go head, man." I laughed with him.

"I'm glad you told me this, cuz she on the way in the door, and I ain't wanna have y'all pretending and shit."

He looked up, and and so did I when Passion and Mary walked in. Passion looked at me with raised eyebrows, probably wondering what was up.

"Hey, True." Mary smiled and sat down.

Guy laughed then grabbed her up and kissed her. Shit, it wasn't a secret anymore, so I kissed the fuck outta Passion.

"True"

"We good?" I said, looking at Mary and Guy.

"Daddy, it's not gon' be the same," she said to Guy.

"I already know that. Y'all hungry because we fucked it up already," he replied to her.

"I could eat, but you know I gotta have some pasta. So,

since we're in New York, we can all have a proper dinner at one of my favorite places, The Spotted Pig." Mary took down the rest of Guy's beer.

"It's a date." Passion looked over at me, and I couldn't help but smile at her happy ass. Shorty was good.

"Aww, look how he looks at her." Mary interrupted the eye lock Passion and I shared.

Passion got in the car with me when we left the burger spot.

"Oh my God, I'm glad they approve. I didn't wanna fight with them again about who I love." She grabbed my hand.

"So, I mean, it's legit now. You officially mine. We gotta celebrate the New Freezer way." I grabbed her hand and let all my niggas know what was up.

"So, I guess it's time to let Chino know, huh?"

"Guess so." I sped off so I could show her something.

I lived a nice distance, so we smoked until we got to my brownstone.

"Whose house is this?" she asked as she got out.

"Mine." I got out and opened the passenger door for her.

"I thought you lived in that party palace." She giggled.

"Nah, nobody but my fam knows where I really live, and now you." I went up and unlocked the door for her.

"Oh my God, True." Passion walked through, smiling at everything she saw.

"I would be spending more time here." She looked around.

"I will be, once I get me a wife. I ain't got no reason for this big ass house." I stopped once she pulled my arm.

"True, I still don't know you as much as somebody in love should, but—"

"You in love with me?" I asked, glad I wasn't crazy about how I was feeling.

"It's no other way to explain how I feel just thinking about you. When I ran into you at my house in Philly, I think I fell in love then," she said with tears.

I caught them and snatched her ass up to me.

"You better make sure you ready, shorty, cuz I play for muthafuckin' keeps."

I kissed her hard and rough then took her ass upstairs and tried my best to get her ass pregnant. When I woke up, I looked at the picture of Gia I kept on my dresser and felt like she was smiling at me.

"I ain't replacing you, ma. I just found somebody I love like I loved you." I kissed her picture and set it back down.

"And don't worry," I heard Passion say behind me. She walked up to the picture. "I'ma love him like you did too." She rubbed Gia's picture, and I broke into tears. I never let anybody see me cry, but Passion had a nigga.

"I miss her," I said as I held onto Passion.

"I know." She held me like nobody was ever able to.

I closed my eyes and clung to her. This moment made me realize she was definitely the one.

YANAI SAT in front of me crying and begging me not to leave her alone.

"I'm sorry, but I got a legit shorty now, and this shit is over with us. I can pay for the rest of your schooling and shit since I promised you, but that's it," I said as she sat in the driver seat of her car crying.

I had met her at Outback so we could eat and talk and shit.

"But, why didn't you choose me? I been good to you!" she screamed.

"Aye, you know the fuck I don't like all that yelling and shit," I barked, and she calmed down. "I ain't sayin' you trash or no shit, but I love her, and that's why I'm with her," I let her know.

"Fine, True. I wasn't shit but pussy, I see." She started her car.

"I'm sorry, aight." I got out, and she sped off without me closing the door.

I felt bad, but I didn't because I was being honest and true to who the fuck I loved.

I got in my truck and pulled off, heading to the house to get ready for Passion's delivery. I knew that money was nothing new to shorty, that's why I ain't winning her with money. I'ma give her the little shit so she knows I see her as more than just some bitch who wanted to be kept. She was my joint now.

I still couldn't believe how I jumped straight into some shit with her. I had hoes that I been fucking with for years who ain't able to make me feel like her. I could see us going a long way. I meant that shit when I said it to her. She was the missing piece in this shit for me. Her ambition and shit made a nigga weak, and she was about business.

Passion was rough around the edges at first, but she was really taking to the shit like she was born with it. I did want her to fall back and keep her hands clean, but baby had her own crew and some more shit, and I knew she wouldn't back down if I asked her. She just wasn't the type.

Once I got home, the truck pulled up right behind me.

"Mr. Luvher?" The fat, white dude jumped out.

"Yeah. Bring it in." I walked through the door and went up to the room I had set up for Passion.

I got her a large pink piano like the one she saw in the mall. The room was painted white with pink and black wall decals featuring inspirational quotes. I had her some lessons set up with one of the best piano instructors in New York, and that nigga wasn't cheap.

I had taken pictures of her laughing while we were at a comedy show the other night and blew them up. They were placed on the walls as well.

The piano fit perfectly in the room too. She was gonna love it. I got a small seat pad for her bench that had her name stitched in it.

I heard the doorbell ring, and I hoped it wasn't passion because I hadn't ordered dinner yet. I was gonna get Uber Eats to bring us some of that good ass barbeque from down the street. I didn't wanna leave at all tonight.

I swung the door open and instantly got pissed off.

"Vee, what the fuck you doin' here?" I said through clenched teeth.

"So, this is where you live?" she had her hands on her hips.

"How the fuck did you find my house?" I asked.

"I can't believe you, True. You ain't think I was good enough to come to your real house after years?" she said in a high pitch screech.

"Man, Passion on the way here. I was gon' wait to holla at you later, but since you stalking me and shit, we fully done, shorty. I'm with her, and I think you should let me know when I'm getting that amnio you tried to throw in my face the other day when you got mad."

"Wow, you really acting brand fucking new because of that hoe." She barged in.

"Get the fuck on, Vee." I went behind her.

"No, let me see if you got a room set up for our baby," she said as she ran up the stairs. She stopped at the room I had for Passion and began to cry.

"Why, True? Look at all you doing. I couldn't get shit—"

"Bitch, don't even fix your mouth to lie. I give you whatever the fuck you want," I barked.

"Except this." She motioned around the house.

"Bye, Vee, man."

"So, you got a room for her and not the baby?" she continued.

"You know what, yeah I do. She mine for sure, but I

don't know if the baby is. When I do, I'll set up a room for my kid. Now, get the fuck out my house, Vee." I pointed.

I heard someone clearing their throat behind me. I turned around to see Passion standing there looking confused. She looked beautiful, though.

"Baby, she barged in here and shit. I'm sorry." I grabbed her and slipped my tongue into her mouth.

"True." Vee started hitting me, and I restrained her.

"Get out my house, Vee. I asked you nice already," I said with a serious look.

"I hate you, nigga!" Vee cried and ran down the stairs.

"Never ending bitches for True," Passion said and squinted into the piano room. "Is that me?"

"Surprise!" I laughed, knowing it was ruined by Vee.

"You did this for me?" She slid her hands over the piano and then the keys.

"Yeah, I got you lessons too. You said you wanted to learn." I sat down on the bench next to her.

"Wow," she said, trying not to look at me.

"You okay?" I turned her head toward me, and she was crying.

"What's wrong?"

"You just so... Ugh, I don't know. You make me feel like exploding, but I'm scared of it."

"I know you are, that's why I'm a love you 'til you not scared."

I kissed her and pulled back, but she pulled me in for more and then grabbed my dick.

"Let's make some music." She grinned and stripped down.

I hurriedly pulled down my jeans.

"Fuck," I said as she slid down on my dick.

Her back hitting the keys as she rode me was sexy as as hell because it ended up sounding like she was playing some shit. I went around to her ass and pushed my finger in.

She screamed and started shaking.

"I'm cumming, fuck." She bounced wildly and realized this would be a quickie when I started cumming too.

"Shit." I came deep inside her.

She ended up getting a birth control thing in her arm or some shit because I had to fuck her raw.

We got cleaned up and went downstairs when her phone started ringing.

"Yeah," she answered and then waited for the reply. "For what?" she asked. "Aight, fuck it, I'm coming." She hung up.

"What good?" I asked.

"Some of the clients wanna meet with me." She looked irritated.

"I'll go with you. I know them niggas," I said, getting up.

"Cool, Pashia said that one dude don't think a lil' bitch could run shit," she said.

"You gon' address that shit," I said and kissed her.

One thing about the streets. Respect was everything, and these niggas needed to respect her. She told me where the meet was at, and I went to Flatbush and parked outside the pizzeria.

"You ready?" I asked, getting out.

"I'm good," she said as she got out.

"Cuz." I saw her cousin coming down the street with the two joints she always stayed with.

"Let's go," Passion simply said and walked in.

I saw the place was packed with people, but we had to head to the basement. I knew the old head who owned the spot. Once we got downstairs, Passion knocked three times, and the small faceplate opened. A pair of eyes looked out, and then the door flew open. I saw Carlo, Davon, Hamp, and Yuri sitting at a table.

"True, we didn't know you would be here," Yuri spoke.

"What's good?" I spoke to them all.

Passion leaned and whispered something to Pashia.

"Okay, so Yuri, since you the chatter box, I want to know what you said about a little bitch not being able to handle her shit." Passion sat across from him.

"What?" he said, obviously lying.

"You heard what the fuck I said," she shot back.

"Look, I knew your pops a long ass time. It's strange for him to send his fuckin' kid up here. You can't stop niggas from even tryna take that lil pussy of yours, lil girl." He slammed his hand on the table.

Passion pulled her gun out and shot him right between the eyes.

"Now that y'all can hear me. I don't give a fuck how you think I should run my shit. If you don't like me, then find somebody else, but oh, you can't. Guess what? Everything coming the fuck through me and my nigga." She pointed at me. "Anybody else gotta problem?" She leaned back.

"We good." They all looked at the lifeless body on the floor.

"This was a short meeting. We could have done this on the phone." Passion got up and walked out the room.

I was gon' fuck her ass into a coma for that shit. Fuck Yuri, he was a rat muthafucka anyway.

CHINO

I don't know what the fuck happened the other night, I was drunk as fuck and ended up over at Passion's spot. She must have called True to come get me, but honestly, I don't even remember that shit. Cherry let me know what happened. I dreamt True knocked my ass out, but I knew he wouldn't do shit like that.

"Cherry, come on, man. The fuck." I barked at her.

"I'm coming, Chino, damn," she yelled back.

I was ready to leave the damn house already, and she been sitting in that damn closet for an hour.

I grabbed my phone and saw my aunt's text that she loved Ronnie. He must have been charming her like his pops. Everybody but Passion knew Ronnie was my son, my family and all. That shit made it hard because my mother would want him and shit when I came through, but she knew if Passion was with me she wouldn't be able to see

169

him. Yeah, she don't agree with how it came about, but he's here, and she was happy about that.

"Damn." Cherry came down with this ugly ass lace dress.

"Bitch, that's all you did? You was up there all that time, I thought you would look better. Go change that ugly shit," I said.

"Fuck you, nigga. You bought the shit." She stomped past me.

"Correction, I paid for it. I would never buy that shit for a hoe." I laughed.

"Whatever. I bet niggas look." She walked to the door.

"Good, cuz I don't wanna see the shit," I teased.

"Man, you ain't been nothing but mean to me since we came out here. What the fuck? You said you wanted to start over," she said, sounding emotionally fucked up.

I was pissed off about Passion, and I was just mad at the world.

"I'm sorry, aight." I kissed her.

She didn't say anything, and I didn't give a fuck.

I walked her out the door, and we came down and got in my Benz.

"Gimme the weed so we can smoke." She held her hand out.

"I told you to grab the shit when you was in the closet," I said, ready to slap the fuck out her.

"I'm sorry." She laughed and got out.

"Fuck it, I'll get it."

I jumped out, knowing it was gon' take her ass all fucking day. I quickly grabbed it and pulled off, knowing I had sheets and a funnel in the console.

By the time we got to True's spot, we had smoked two of them, and I was high as fuck. I was ready to drink and shit now. People were heading in, and damn, I wished I would have left Cherry at home once I saw those bitches.

"Oh, this shit live," Cherry said as she walked through the doors.

"Damn." I looked around at the joint, and it was lit as fuck.

He had strippers and shit. My nigga. I saw Lucci walking over to a couch where True sat.

"What's up, Chino?" Lucci said.

"Wassup? What's good, True?" I sat down next to him.

"Ain't shit. You see what I'm up to, cuz." He poured some 1738 in his cup.

"Fuck yeah," I said and grabbed a cup.

"My baby here." Lucci said, standing up.

I saw Pashia, Passion's cousin walk up with one bad bitch and one ugly ass bitch. Then I saw Passion making it through the crowd.

"Cherry, you funny as fuck. I told Passion the first time I met your ass I ain't like you." Pashia started up. "She boutta spazz on your ass." Pashia said as Passion walked up.

She burst out laughing when she walked up and saw me and Cherry.

"Bitch, what's funny? I should hop on ya ass for fuckin' up my shit," Cherry said.

"You ain't gon' do shit, bitch. I'll have your ass dropped before you reach me." Passion gritted on her.

"You reached a new low. Came begging at my door and had this bitch up here in waiting. Y'all some clowns," Passion continued.

"Shit, you said you wasn't fuckin' with me, shorty. I have to do right by my son." I smirked.

"You better hope Ronnie is yours with as many niggas as she was fuckin'."

"Chino, you knew this bitch was gon' be here?" Cherry yelled.

"No, the fuck I didn't. Matter of fact, the fuck you doin' at my cousin's shit, tho?" I asked.

"Nigga, True said I'm welcome anytime. And my bitches," Passion said as more bitches walked up behind her.

She had changed and quick as fuck on a nigga.

"Come and chill, shorty., True said to Passion.

"Let's dance y'all." Passion smirked, and all them hoes followed her. She ain't pay me or Cherry no fucking attention as she danced and shit.

"When the fuck she start coming around and shit?" I asked True.

"For a minute." He drank down his drink.

"Why you ain't tell me y'all was chillin' and shit?"

"The fuck it matter?" Cherry started again.

"I'm boutta knock you the fuck out in a minute," I said to her ass.

"Nigga, you fuckin' up the vibe," Lucci said.

"True, come here for a minute." Passion ran and pulled him up.

I literally felt my blood boiling when they all started dancing on him and shit. Passion was grinding on the nigga's dick.

"Passion!" I barked.

She threw up her middle finger and continued to twerk on True as he held her waist. I knew the fuck I wasn't trippin.

"The fuck? You tryna fuck my girl, True?" I walked up to them.

"Hold up, nigga. Fuck you talkin' 'bout. I'm your girl, nigga." Cherry popped off behind me.

"Nigga, she ain't your girl no more. Your girl right there next to you. Don't come in my shit playin' wit' me, cuz," True spat.

"So what the fuck you sayin', nigga? You fuckin' her?" I asked.

"What the fuck if I was, nigga? You let her go, nigga. If I was, that really wouldn't be your business no more." True stood up.

"You fuckin' my cousin, bitch?" I said to Passion.

"Nigga, am I? In every part of my house, and that couch you was sitting on." She cackled, and I went toward her, but I heard several guns cocking behind me and beside me.

I saw the bitches she came with, including her cousin, with guns on me.

"Chill, he's my blood, y'all," True said for them to lower the guns.

"That's fucked up, cuz."

I swung on True, and he dodged me and caught me across the face.

We started tussling, and the nigga was giving me go. My cousin always had hands.

"You fighting over this bitch!" Cherry yelled and started hitting me.

I stopped fighting True to slap the fuck out that bitch.

"Nigga, you foul as fuck. You supposed to be my blood," I said to True.

"Nigga, what the fuck you mean? I always looked out for your ass, cuz. You emotional as fuck, and you need to roll up out my shit, nigga," True said, taking his shirt off.

"Nigga, fuck you. I'm taking Ronnie and leaving.

"SHUT THE FUCK UP! I DON'T GIVE A FUCK WHERE YOU GO, JUST GET THE FUCK OUT MY FACE!" I screamed at Cherry.

I looked at Passion and nodded then walked out the front door. I knew I wasn't fucking tripping about that shit when I called True. That nigga smiled all in my fucking face, and was fucking Passion behind my back. I didn't know if it was Karma for the shit I did back in the day, or what.

I tried to rob True's house with my friend, Bruce, but

nobody was supposed to be there. Gia saw us, and I had to kill her ass because True would kill me if he found out. I even had to kill Bruce ass too.

"I fuckin' hate you, Chino!" I heard Cherry scream from down the street.

I wasn't worried about that bitch. I jumped in my car and sped off fast as shit. I was so pissed I was seeing colors and shit. Once I realized the colors were sirens behind me, I pulled over. The officer walked up and flashed the light in my face. I rolled the window down.

"You know why I pulled you over?" he asked.

"How the fuck I'm supposed to know? I look like a mind reader?" I asked.

"You need to calm down," he said like he was ready to unload on my ass. "You were going one ten."

"It goes to two twenty."

All I could think about was Passion fucking True, and that shit had my head gone. I sped off while he stood there and cut down several streets to make sure he couldn't catch up. But then, one was coming my way with his lights, and he bucked a U on my ass and chased me. I was caught dead locked in traffic.

"Fuck," I said when they pulled up behind me.

"You need to be back for your hearing," the judge said after I was granted bail.

I was in there for three days, and I was still hot as fuck. I was taken back until my bail was posted, but I didn't even call no fucking body. Maybe I needed to be in this bitch right now because I felt like I would be right back. True knew how the fuck I felt about Passion. That girl was my life, and he fucking knew the shit.

"Luvher, come on," the guard called out after a few minutes.

"What's up?" I asked.

"Somebody posted for you," he said as he opened the cell.

"Who bailed me out?" I asked.

"Don't know, don't care," he replied.

I got processed out, and when I made it out front, I saw True standing there.

"Get the fuck in," he said.

"Nigga, fuck you, cuz. That shit foul, man. I ain't never do you dirty," I lied.

"Nigga, shut the fuck up and get in. This ain't got shit to do with Passion," he said.

The back window rolled down, and I saw Passion's father in the back.

True got in the Hummer, and I skeptically got in behind him.

"The fuck you doin' here?" I asked William.

"Tryin' hard not to lay hands on you for fuckin' with my daughter," he replied.

I had only met him when Passion was arguing to get away from them when we were younger.

"The fuck type of bullshit you on, True?" I said, ignoring William.

"Muthafucka, I'm talkin' to you." The nigga pulled the strap.

"Passion did some foul shit with this nigga," I said to him.

"Nigga, you the foulest of them all." He put his gun away. "You think my daughter your mufuckin' play thing, nigga. She moved the fuck on and you need to do the same fuckin' thing. You lucky your cousin spoke up for you because I wasn't feeling the shit I heard about you from jump. So, nigga, get this through your head. My daughter is no longer a part of Chino Luvher. You feel me? Forget her, move the fuck on with that bucket head STD infected bitch Cherry you knocked up. I don't wanna hear shit else from my daughter about you, feel me?" he said as we turned a corner.

"It's all good. That was my plan. Fuck it," I said, looking at True. I felt betrayed to the highest level.

"You can let us out," True said as we pulled up to the train station.

True jumped out, and so did I.

"So, the fuck was that nigga supposed to do, scare me?" I said.

"Nigga, you should be. Look, that shit with Passion, man, she my shorty now, point, blank period. All that shit with y'all is in the past. I know it seem foul but it wasn't my intention. You my blood, and I love you, nigga, but anything having to do with her is on me now," he said with his arms folded.

"That's still foul as fuck. But it's all gravy, nigga," I said and walked off from him.

I didn't give a fuck about that nigga or William's threats. I was gonna get my pay back. Fuck 'em all.

2 *MONTHS later*

"I now pronounce you man and wife," I heard the judge say as Cherry and I got married in the courthouse. We kissed and turned to all her ugly ass people and my family sitting there. True didn't come, but some other New Freezer niggas showed up. I mean, it wasn't like I invited him and shit, but hey, the nigga knew what time it was.

It was gon take me a minute to get over Passion, and he knew that shit. I mean, we been slightly cordial because at the end of the day, we are blood. But I ain't fucking with him like that.

"I love you." Cherry kissed me."

"Love you too," I said and half meant it.

"My baby." Ma came up and hugged me.

My aunt Gabbie was there, and she also came up and hugged me.

"Thanks, y'all." I smiled.

I married Cherry because her ass fucked around and got

knocked up again. She was only five weeks, but the bitch acted like she was nine months already.

"Oh my God!!" I heard my Aunt Gabbie scream.

"What's wrong?" My mother ran over and looked at the phone.

I ran over and saw a live video of True proposing to Passion on a boat. The surrounding area looked like an island or something.

"You gon' marry me, baby? I can't wait another day," True said.

"Yes, True!" Passion screamed.

All the attention on me and Cherry was gone as everybody stood around and watched the video.

Once me and Cherry were safely on the flight to Jamaica for our honeymoon, all I could think about was Passion and True. That shit was still eating me the fuck up. She broke my heart with this shit. That bitch wanna hurt me, so I'ma hurt her ass.

PASSION

*M*y stupid ass was still sitting there crying and looking at my ring.

"I can't believe you, True. How can you wanna marry me? I'm scared, baby. You serious?" I said all in one breath.

"Yes, girl. You gonna be my wife. King of New Freezer and Queen of Dirty Diamond Girls. It's meant to be. We gon' run every fuckin' thing," True said as he held me.

"How can you love me like this?" I smiled as the music started and he swayed me.

"How can I not?" he said and kissed me.

We danced and danced for what seemed like hours. It really was hours when I realized two and a half had passed.

"Let's get back on the island," True called up to the Mexican man who drove the yacht.

"True," I said, not believing it.

"I know, baby. I think time is just a state of mind. It don't matter how long I've loved you, as long as I do right."

"You so fire."

I kissed him, and we lay on the deck in a hammock until we reached land. He carried me off the dock once we got back to land.

"I love you, Passion. The sooner we plan this wedding the better. I'm anxious." He smiled and laid me on the bed of the bungalow.

"Passion Luvher." I laughed.

"I'm a Passion luvher." His cheesy ass kissed my belly and proceeded down to my pussy.

"Baby," I moaned as he licked on my pussy.

"That's right, shorty. Shit boutta get real." He slid his tongue into my pussy while playing with my clit.

"Shit, shit, shit." I could never hold out on him; he got me quick as fuck.

"Now, turn over. I'ma make your ass scream."

And he damn sure did, all damn night. Island police came and checked on us because of the noise. We fell asleep wet and satisfied, and most importantly, in love.

"COME ON, MA." True said, hurrying me off the jet.

"I'm sorry, these heels hurt. You made me wear them," I reminded his ass.

"Cuz you look good as fuck in them," he said and squinted to keep the sun out of his eyes.

"Thanks," I said and posed.

He loaded the bags into the car then helped me inside. I quickly kicked them damn heels off.

I didn't want to leave my baby, but he said he had moves to make. When he dropped me off, I was sad as hell. It was cool, though. He never stayed away too long. I took a shower and decided to take a nap. Hopefully, True would be done doing whatever his ass was doing by the time I woke up. He was heavy in these streets, and it was sexy as hell to see him sticking and moving because he did it with such swag.

I rolled a jay so it would make me tired. I didn't get to sleep on the flight, so this shit right should do just fine.

As soon as I started smoking, my phone began to ring off the hook. Since True went live, quite a few family members were calling to give congrats. I saw that it was Alexandria.

"Hey, Alex," I said when I picked up.

"They dead!" she cried.

"What? Who dead?" I screamed.

"Mother and Father!"

"NOOOO! NOOOOO!!!!!

I sat in my black dress and watched the caskets being lowered into the grown together. I had been crying for six days straight, and nobody had any answers. How could my father and mother be dead? The loss was real in my chest.

"I'm sorry, baby," True said as he held me.

"Thank you for being here," I told him.

Alexandria lay in Mark's arms sobbing as well. This shit was surreal.

After the burial, I sat in the repast looking like a zombie. People were coming up to me, and I couldn't even speak.

"I'm sorry about this, Passion." Chino came up with Cherry.

"Me too." Cherry looked at me sincerely.

"Why y'all here?" I looked at them.

"Baby." True held my arm.

"I just wanted to offer my condolences." Chino came down to hug me. "And to see that look on your face when I tell you I killed them," he whispered and walked away with Cherry in tow.

To be continued...

Social Media
Facebook- Ebony Diamond Turrentine
Group- Just chill with Ebony
 Diamonds
Instagram- authoress_Ebony_diamonds
Twitter- @ebonydiamonds86

Made in the USA
Columbia, SC
02 May 2025

57451866R00114